PENGUIN BOOKS

The Rainfall Market

You Yeong-Gwang was born in Seongnam in 1984. He wrote this story during breaks while delivering food for a living. He felt truly happy while writing this story and wishes for all readers to find healing and courage through it so that they may go out and find their own happiness. *The Rainfall Market* was a runaway bestseller in Korea selling over one hundred thousand copies and has been sold in fifteen languages.

The Rainfall Market

YOU YEONG-GWANG

Translated by Slin Jung

PENGUIN BOOKS

PENGUIN BOOKS

UK | USA | Canada | Ireland | Australia
India | New Zealand | South Africa

Penguin Books is part of the Penguin Random House group of companies whose addresses can be found at global.penguinrandomhouse.com

Penguin Random House UK,
One Embassy Gardens, 8 Viaduct Gardens, London SW11 7BW

penguin.co.uk

First published in Korea as The Rainbow Goblin Store by Clayhouse 2023
First published in Great Britain by Penguin Michael Joseph 2024
Published by Penguin Books 2025

003

Copyright © You Yeong-Gwang, 2023
English translation copyright © Slin Jung, 2024

Contents page image © Jedit (@9jedit); Serin character image © Tithi Luadthong, Shutterstock; Issha character image by Lady Zhegalova via Pixabay; Mata & Popo character images by Dmitry Abramov via Pixabay; all other character images by LeoNeoBoy via Pixabay

This book is published with the support of the Literature Translation Institute of Korea (LTI Korea)

The moral right of the author has been asserted

Penguin Random House values and supports copyright. Copyright fuels creativity, encourages diverse voices, promotes freedom of expression and supports a vibrant culture. Thank you for purchasing an authorized edition of this book and for respecting intellectual property laws by not reproducing, scanning or distributing any part of it by any means without permission. You are supporting authors and enabling Penguin Random House to continue to publish books for everyone. No part of this book may be used or reproduced in any manner for the purpose of training artificial intelligence technologies or systems. In accordance with Article 4(3) of the DSM Directive 2019/790, Penguin Random House expressly reserves this work from the text and data mining exception

Set in 11/13pt Dante MT Std
Typeset by Six Red Marbles UK, Thetford, Norfolk
Printed and bound in Great Britain by Clays Ltd, Elcograf S.p.A.

The authorized representative in the EEA is Penguin Random House Ireland, Morrison Chambers, 32 Nassau Street, Dublin D02 YH68

A CIP catalogue record for this book is available from the British Library

ISBN: 978-1-405-96468-5

Penguin Random House is committed to a sustainable future for our business, our readers and our planet. This book is made from Forest Stewardship Council® certified paper.

Characters

Serin

A girl who wants to escape her dreary life

Invited to a mysterious market that only opens during the rainy season, Serin is caught up in a whirlwind of adventures. She wanders the Rainfall Market in search of happiness.

Issha

A guide cat who follows the holder of the Golden Ticket

A spirit creature who looks like a cat but acts like a puppy. Issha changes size at will and guides Serin to the Dokkaebi stores that keep the futures she wants.

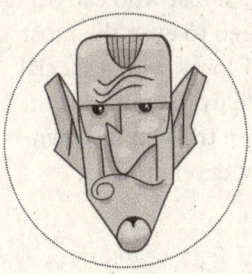

Toriya

The Rainfall Market gatekeeper

Although he is a mountain of a man with fists the size of boulders, Toriya is meek and gentle, and does odd jobs for the Rainfall Market. He is afraid of insects and adores flowers.

Durof

The guide to the Rainfall Market

With his immaculate purple suit and pomade-slicked hair, Durof collects people's stories and invites guests to the Rainfall Market.

Berna

Manager of the Misfortune Pawnshop

Though she looks mean-tempered and impossible to please, Berna always gets the job done and never drops so much as a number. An avid smoker, she purchases people's misfortunes at reasonable prices to keep the pawnshop afloat.

Emma

The Hair Salon's senior stylist

An eager hair stylist who can bring a glossy sheen to even the most damaged of locks with a special hair oil made from compliments, Emma often trips on her own blow-dryer cords.

Mata

The owner of the Ruined Bookshop

A shy young Dokkaebi who just turned a hundred years old, Mata loves books and tearfully ponders what he could steal from human hearts. He was formerly friends with Haku the troublemaker.

Bordo

Chef at the Giants' Restaurant

Though constantly arguing with his younger brother, everyone agrees that his cooking is second to none. His special ingredient? A mysterious sauce made of forgotten human memories.

Popo

The gardener at the mischief-tree grove

An elderly Dokkaebi who brings flowers into bloom and raises towering trees with the sweat and tears humans shed in pursuit of their goals. She knows the secret about Rainbow Orbs.

The Perfumery's master artisan

Specializing in perfumes made with essence of human words, Nicole also sells stink sprays and scented candles. The explosions from her lab can be heard from across the Market.

Nicole

Manager of the Pyramid Casino

Stealing away people's desire to sleep at night, Gromm runs a booming round-the-clock casino. Unfortunately, he sometimes steals a little too much and falls asleep on the job.

Gromm

Master of the Rainfall Market

The legendary creator of the Rainfall Market, Yan works closely with the Misfortune Pawnshop. He is the owner of the VIP lounge and lives in the penthouse at the top of the Market.

Yan

Contents

	Prologue	xi
1.	The Strange Rumour	1
2.	The Strange Letter	8
3.	The Heatwave	15
4.	The First Night of the Rainy Season	21
5.	The Gatekeeper	27
6.	The Rainfall Market	33
7.	The Misfortune Pawnshop	39
8.	The Information Desk	47
9.	The Hair Salon	54
10.	The Bookshop	68
11.	The Perfumery	80
12.	The Garden	93
13.	The Restaurant	106
14.	The Curiosity Shop	121
15.	The Scrap Yard	129
16.	The Casino	137
17.	The Dungeon	152
18.	The Lounge Bar	164
19.	The Penthouse	170

20.	Issha the Guide Cat	177
21.	The Treasure Vault	182
22.	The Rainbow	190
	Epilogue	195
	Afterword	197

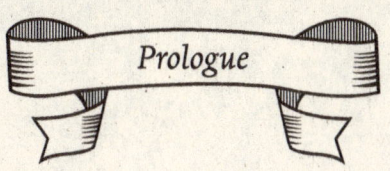

Prologue

Crackle . . . hiss . . .

'Ugh, not again.'

Serin smacked the old radio impatiently; she was tired of trying to coax it back into working.

Miraculously, the weatherman's voice returned to the speakers: 'Due to the high-pressure front over the North Pacific, rainfall is expected over the entire Korean Peninsula next week . . .'

Serin nearly dropped the poor old radio.

It was finally here. The rainy season, and with it the answer to her prayers: the Rainfall Market.

Episode 1
The Strange Rumour

Somewhere far outside the big city was a place called Rainbow Town.

And somewhere in Rainbow Town was a run-down, abandoned house.

Rumour had it if you sent a letter about your misfortune to this house, you would receive a mysterious Ticket. If you brought that ticket to the house on the first day of the rainy season, you could completely change your life.

'No way.'

'That's absolutely ridiculous.'

Everyone treated it as a fantasy at first. But somehow, the story spread like wildfire. And each time it was told, it became more and more elaborate.

But though the details were different, they all had one thing in common. The Dokkaebi.

'I swear, I saw them with my own eyes!'

The people who claimed to have visited the house insisted that behind its doors was a secret, magical world with beings who called themselves Dokkaebi: people who looked human, but weren't.

'Don't make me laugh.'

Naturally, people didn't believe those stories so easily. But Serin wasn't the only one who wanted to know more. Most people snickered when they heard about these Dokkaebi and their Tickets, but Serin would pause with her spoon halfway to her mouth so she could learn more from the rumours. She even borrowed *Secrets of the Rainfall Market* at the school library, which was no easy feat considering how popular it was. Serin skipped lunch that day, and with the precious book finally in her hands, rushed to a corner of the library.

Even the cover of the book was special. The publisher had obviously spared no expense, from the way the cover changed colour when Serin held it up to the light at different angles. She stared at the cover for what seemed like forever. There was the heart-stopping quote, *The truth behind the rumours finally revealed!* and most importantly, the bright red *BEST-SELLER* mark stamped on the front. Serin hated books, but she couldn't pass this one by. She could tell other people thought the same, because the book was already badly worn, even though it had just been published.

Taking a deep breath, she gingerly opened the book.

'Ugh, really?'

Printed on the front flap was a picture of the author. He was smiling like a robot, and someone had drawn glasses over his eyes and blackened some of his teeth with a permanent marker, so it was impossible to tell what he actually looked like.

The rest of the book wasn't much better. Serin found doodles, of course, and even phone numbers and email addresses people had jotted down in a rush. The pencilled underlinings, she could tolerate. But some of the pages clung together with something yellow and sticky, and Serin had to try very hard to pretend not to notice those. *I'm only here for information!*

Despite all that, the book gripped her from the start. In the introduction, the author wrote about how he had gained entry to the Rainfall Market. He explained that his life had been hopeless once and he was often in and out of prison.

He used to be as sad as I am, Serin thought.

Each time he was released from prison, the author wrote, he had wanted to make a fresh start. But because no one would hire someone with his past, he had nowhere to go and was completely destitute.

Everything changed the day he picked up a newspaper to look for job ads. He spotted the words *Tell us about your misfortune*, and an address. The man had nothing left to lose. He poured out his heart on paper and sent it off by mail. To his shock, he heard back: he found a Ticket in the letterbox, alongside an invitation to a strange marketplace.

Serin wondered if she might get a Ticket. She tried to compare her life with the author's, but it was hard to tell who had it worse.

Before she knew it, she was halfway through the book. Across the chapters, the author described the Dokkaebi he met and the wonders of the Rainfall Market. He had even included maps, almost like a travel guide. At the end of the book, the author described how he had chosen a new, happy future for himself at the Market, and how that happy life came to be. He had always wanted to be a famous writer. And not long after he had finished writing the manuscript for *Secrets of the Rainfall Market*, he won a deal with the biggest publishing house in the industry. The rest was history. But while helpful, that information wasn't quite what Serin was after.

'This is it!'

The appendix in the back had everything she'd wanted. It was the whole reason she'd borrowed the book in the first place. She turned the page and saw a list of tips for sending a good letter, one that would get chosen. The writer swore that he had spoken with other human visitors to verify these tips. This was the real deal.

'Where did I put my pen?'

Serin pulled out a small notepad and copied down everything the appendix had to say about getting her letter accepted.

It was better to be honest rather than embellish too much. Believe it or not, the author warned, Dokkaebi could read people's hearts, so they could tell if someone was lying. He said that the Dokkaebi didn't care as much about your writing skills as they did about your circumstances.

But is all this really real?

At the very end of the appendix, the author wrote that the Rainfall Market had changed his life when all seemed hopeless, and that if anyone reading his book felt the way he did, they had nothing to lose by writing to the Dokkaebi.

Back in the classroom, Serin could not concentrate.

And not because her teacher, who insisted on wearing modernized hanbok clothing all year round, had a big hole near his underarm. Or because part of his comb-over was hanging limp off the side, exposing his balding head.

She couldn't stop thinking about *the book*.

The blackboard was almost completely white with chalk, and the teacher was lecturing passionately about history – or geography, she couldn't quite tell – with thick drops of spittle flying everywhere. But Serin's mind was on the Rainfall Market.

It can't possibly be real, she told herself. She had to focus on her lessons. But shaking her head didn't help, and only attracted the teacher's attention.

'Kim Serin, are you listening to me?'

The teacher was looking straight at her. Serin gasped. 'I-I'm sorry, sir.'

The teacher frowned and pulled his comb-over back over his head, then pushed up his horn-rimmed glasses and continued the lesson. But the chalks kept breaking, and he ended up getting mad at the blackboard, ranting about how people didn't make things like they used to.

It felt like he was talking to her. Serin hung her head, her face bright red.

A few of her classmates glanced in her direction, but no one tried to console her. She was used to that by now.

When she got home, Serin turned on her desk lamp and, as usual, shuffled through the radio channels to find her favourite music programme.

The radio was probably once a classy bright red, but it had faded to the colour of pink rubber gloves. For a long time, it had worked surprisingly well. But recently, the old machine had needed a bit of encouragement from Serin's hand.

'Why does it keep acting up?'

She had a good reason for keeping the battered old radio, though: it was the last thing she had left of her father's.

Serin didn't remember her father. All she knew was that he died suddenly in an accident when she was young. Her mother had tried to throw the radio away many times, but Serin had insisted on keeping it.

It was her only friend. A member of the family who filled the void in her heart.

At ten in the evening, the radio played the opening song of her favourite programme.

'Good evening. Welcome to another nightly episode of *The Dream Box*.'

Serin loved the DJ's soft, soothing voice, and normally pricked up her ears for the entire show. But not today. She placed a piece of writing paper she'd picked up on the way home on her desk, and fell deep into thought with her chin on her hands. Her pen twirled round and round in her fingers before clattering to the desktop.

'Now for our next segment: Stories from the Listeners.'

Serin had never been the best writer. She'd written to the show many times, but they never picked her. As hope gave way to disappointment again and again, she learned that it was easier to just give up altogether.

The show went on, and eventually, Serin sat up straight. She had to do this.

The circled date on her desktop calendar said exams were coming up next week. But she could start thinking about them tomorrow. Right now, she had to focus on writing her letter. Serin looked from her notepad to her writing paper and trawled through her memories.

I'm supposed to be honest, right?

Putting pen to paper, Serin began to write. She wrote about how she lived alone with her mother, how they had already been poor before their old house caught fire and forced them to move into a semi-basement apartment with precious little sunlight. How she didn't have money for a school uniform, and had to get hand-me-downs. How her little sister Yerin had run away from home last year and was still missing.

Serin didn't worry about whether her letter was confusing or if the wording was poor. She wrote it all down, even the things she was too embarrassed to talk about.

'Thank you for sharing that heartbreaking story with us. I'm sure it couldn't have been easy. My advice is to stop blaming yourself, because you have endured more than anyone.'

As the radio went on in the background, Serin poured her heart out. When she looked up, it was almost morning. She folded up the writing paper, placed it in an envelope, and then lay down on the floor on a frayed old blanket.

Curled up asleep next to her was her mother. Serin hadn't even noticed her come in. She must have come home in the middle of the night after her shift at the restaurant and gone to sleep quietly because she thought Serin was studying.

Keeping her earphones in, Serin brought the radio down to the floor. It was playing her favourite song: 'A Tomorrow Better Than Today'. She'd sung along so often that just the first few notes had her automatically mouthing the words.

'It may feel like it's raining. But don't forget that there's always a silver lining in every cloud . . .'

Finally, Serin closed her eyes.

Perhaps it was the sweet melody or that she was she simply that tired, but as soon as her head hit the pillow, she fell into a deep sleep.

Episode 2
The Strange Letter

She hadn't hoped for much.

Serin knew that the more she hoped, the worse the disappointment would be. She wasn't really desperate to go to the Rainfall Market. It was more of a dream, a vague hope that she might escape her terrible life.

Or maybe she just wanted to see if the rumours were true.

Oh well, that's just who I am.

It had been nearly two months. Her grades dropped a little because of exams, but Serin didn't mind. She had no chance of saving enough for university anyway. And even though her mother didn't say so, she probably thought it was best for Serin to start working as soon as possible to help the family.

After classes, the other students went off to expensive crammers in their little cliques. Serin was the only one who headed home. It was even in the opposite direction.

Her steps slowed. Serin sighed as she looked up at the endless steps that led up the hillside. They were so steep that even healthy young people like her had to be careful in rain or snow, and in the summer, she couldn't reach the top without getting drenched in sweat. She hated these steps almost as much as she hated sitting bored in school.

Panting, she finally reached a plateau carved into the hill, which sat almost level with the tops of high-rise condos in the distance. This was the entrance to her neighbourhood, which was mostly made up of grey houses clustered together in rows, broken up by tiny alleyways barely big enough for one person at a time. Because so many of the roofs were leaky, they were covered with orange tarpaulins held down by motley collections of tyres and old roof tiles. They would keep the tarpaulins secure even in strong winds and typhoons, hopefully.

'Hey, it's my turn!'

Because it was still afternoon, the alleyways were deserted, except for the children who were too young to go to school. A group of little boys whose shirts barely covered anything had piled up a heap of sand and stuck a branch on top, and were taking turns removing sand from the heap. A second later, they spotted an old man hauling up a cart full of junk and scampered over to him, not even wiping the snot from their noses. One of the boys tripped and fell, bursting into tears.

'Careful now, boys!' warned the old man, dressed in shorts and a sleeveless jacket for the summer. He beamed as he hugged the excited children. Lovingly, he called them 'you rascals' and told them to move out of the way. The rascals crowded around the back of the cart to help push it up the hill – even though they probably wouldn't make much of a difference.

Serin let the cart pass first before stepping into the alleyway herself.

'Meooooow!'

The second she set foot in the alley, she heard a pitiful noise.

Serin scanned her surroundings and spotted a pair of eyes in a tiny gap between the houses. Slowly, she approached the little creature.

'Hey there. Are you hungry?'

As if in response, the cat mewled again.

Serin rummaged through her pockets. She'd long since run out of pocket money, but maybe she had something – and luckily, her fingers found a handful of coins.

Could I buy anything with this? she wondered, looking from the coins to the cat and back again. She quickly got to her feet and headed for the corner store.

The corner store was a tiny place and the neighbourhood elders' favourite haunt. The blue sign read 'Supermarket', but it was missing so many letters that it barely counted as a sign. Even the sticker that read 'Tobacco' had long since faded to a blur.

The old woman who ran the store wasn't even at the counter. Instead, she sat on the platform outside the building with a group of friends who were busy playing Go-stop with their cards. She wasn't playing, though. She just made comments to the old woman next to her about which card to play next, occasionally snacking on a piece of Korean melon. Only when she spotted Serin enter the store did she heave herself down from the platform.

'What'll it be, dearie?' she asked, pulling the elastic waistband of her trousers all the way up to her chest.

'Do you have anything a cat could eat?'

'A pussycat, now?'

'Right.'

'And would this be a street cat? Or a housecat?'

'A street cat,' Serin replied, holding up a slender fish sausage.

The old woman tut-tutted. 'You can't just feed it any old human snack. Wait here a minute.' She went back outside, picked up a few pieces of melon, pulled off the seeds, and put the melon into a black plastic bag. 'Try these, dear. Better than that factory-made stuff.'

Serin smiled for the first time in what seemed like forever. 'Thank you, ma'am!'

Bowing again and again, Serin rushed out of the corner store. The old woman beamed at her, then went back to the platform to play more armchair Go-stop.

Though she was walking as fast as she could, Serin was worried. What if the cat had disappeared while she was gone?

Thankfully, the cat was still there in its little hiding place, but now it was meowing even more loudly in her direction. Serin first showed it the plastic bag and opened it up so the cat could take a sniff. Its ears twitched at every rustle of the bag. She wanted more than anything to get closer and feed the cat out of her palm, but she didn't want to scare the poor thing. So she took several steps back, squatted, and held out a piece of melon in her fingers.

The cat stared warily for a moment, reaching a hesitant paw before withdrawing it, then reaching out and withdrawing again, but finally ventured out of the hole all the way until the tip of its tail was in the light. It grabbed the melon in its mouth and rushed back inside.

In that moment, Serin noticed that although the cat was mostly skinny, it had a strangely large belly.

Oh, it's pregnant.

Serin stared into the darkness. Then she placed the plastic bag in the little gap between the houses there. She didn't want the cat to get sick eating spoiled food out of the rubbish. If she could, she would have taken the cat home to keep. But her mother would definitely not let her. She said no to anything that might cost even a little bit of money.

'I hope you have healthy kittens,' Serin said longingly, and went on her way.

★

Serin and her mother lived in an old apartment building that had been split further into tiny single units. Pasted in big letters on the building wall was a notice saying the building was due for demolition, and spray-painted gossip about who was dating who, and who was looking for a girlfriend.

None of it was new to her. But the vivid red envelope in the letterbox was. Serin stopped in her tracks, because almost no one ever sent them mail.

For a moment, she wondered if it was another debt collection notice that she should ignore. But then she remembered it was better not to let other people see it, so she picked the envelope out of the letterbox.

It was not a debt collection notice.

The envelope was covered in strange symbols. Then her eyes were drawn to the golden seal, which wouldn't be out of place in some European palace.

From: THE RAINFALL MARKET

Serin had to read the recipient line again. The letter was most certainly addressed to her unit. To her name. Confused and excited all at once, she rushed down the stairs. Her heart pounded louder and faster than she'd imagined possible.

Not even taking her shoes off at the door, Serin tore open the envelope and its almost too-beautiful seal.

Scrawled in elegant, looping letters was the following message:

Dear Ms Kim Serin,

Thank you for sending us your story.
Honesty and trust are the pillars on which the Rainfall Market is built, and each year we uphold our proud tradition of providing our customers with only the best in service.

Without further ado, we at the Rainfall Market are delighted to extend you an exclusive offer in exchange for your story.

Would you be interested in selling us your misfortune?

At the Rainfall Market, you will have the chance to trade in your misfortune for a happier story in our stock.

Should you wish to accept our invitation, please bring the enclosed Ticket to the address on the envelope on the first day of the rainy season. Depending on the length of this year's rainy season, your stay with us may last up to two weeks.

As customer satisfaction and comfort are our highest priorities, your stay and meals will be fully covered by the Rainfall Market.

We hope to welcome you in person soon.

(Please note that we do not take responsibility for any trouble that may occur at the Rainfall Market.)

Serin clamped a hand over her mouth, stifling a squeal. There it was, in the envelope, the Ticket mentioned in the letter. It was small, and the same shiny gold as the fancy seal.

Wait, did the book say the Ticket was golden? Serin tried to remember what she'd read, but she hadn't paid much attention to that part. *Oh well,* she thought, and looked back at the letter.

She hadn't expected much, but now that the Ticket was in her hands, she couldn't believe it. She wanted to pinch herself, just to make sure she wasn't dreaming, but she knew that would only leave an ugly red mark.

Something did bother her, though. The last line of the letter.

Why wouldn't they take responsibility for any trouble?

She'd once heard that the police had arrested a gang that had been luring people with the promise of work, only to sell their organs on the black market. And the yellowed newspaper she and her mother used for wallpaper prominently displayed an article about a man who had been kept as a slave on an island village, rescued years after being taken.

Serin paced around the room, biting her thumb, and fidgeted in every way she knew in the tiny apartment. But she just couldn't decide.

As she spoke aloud all the reasons she should or shouldn't go, she finally screamed, 'Well, why not? The book said it was real!'

The Ticket crumpled a little in her hand. Serin jumped and rushed up to the battered bookshelf across the room, took out the biggest book she could find, and slid the Ticket between the pages. Still not satisfied, she put the book down and then stacked her textbooks on top of that.

What if I really could change my life?

She went up to the opening that barely counted as a window. The sliver of sky was the size of her hand, but it was such a beautiful, clear blue.

I wonder when the rain will start?

It was still springtime, with not a cloud in the sky. The rainy season seemed like an eternity away.

Episode 3
The Heatwave

'Well, if it isn't Serin! Where are you off to now?' asked a lady with curls so tight they must have been freshly done. The woman was in her mid-forties, and wore a purple T-shirt tight enough to make everyone else feel the summer heat.

'Taekwondo lessons,' Serin said, making no effort to hide her annoyance.

Oblivious, the woman fanned herself as she came up to Serin, fingering those fresh curls with her other hand. 'Oh sweetheart, you're better off studying instead! And girls shouldn't be wasting time with something so boorish,' she crooned irritatingly, and shifted her bag of groceries to her other shoulder. 'You know what they say, a girl's best off keeping quietly to her books until she finds herself a good marriage. You've suffered enough, dear.'

'Okay. I have to go now, ma'am,' Serin said tersely, and strode away briskly. The woman seemed to have more to say, but tut-tutted as her prey escaped.

Three times a week, Serin went in for afterschool taekwondo lessons. It was the only extracurricular activity she did. Lessons were already cheap because the classes were state-funded, but Serin was so badly off that she was exempt from even the discounted fees.

Although she rushed as fast as she could to the dojo, everyone else must have already got ready, because she could hear their yells from outside the door.

'Late again, Kim Serin. Keep this up and you might have to do extra drills,' teased the master, who was on the younger side.

Serin put on an apologetic face. 'I'm sorry, sir,' she said, scratching her head. Then she ran so quickly to the changing rooms that her hair streamed in the air behind her. She put on her uniform.

A second before she left, though, she took a glance at the mirror. In her bright white uniform, she looked almost brave. Not like when she was in her ill-fitting hand-me-down school clothes.

Once she'd tied her belt neatly over her top and let the ends hang loose, she found herself smiling. She was only a red belt now, but once she passed the exam, she would add a black stripe to her belt, which was practically a black belt.

Fixing her uniform once more, Serin stepped on to the dojo floor just in time to hear the master go over the day's exercises.

'Like I said last week, we'll be breaking real boards today. But don't get too scared, as we'll be using pine boards because it's only practice.'

Serin gulped. She'd been looking forward to the exercise for what seemed like forever.

A long time ago, she'd happened to see a taekwondo demonstration on TV, with people doing flips in midair as they broke wooden boards. When she realized that some of those practitioners were women, Serin's heart raced. It was like a huge wave rising from deep inside, and she simply had to know more. When she learned that there was an afterschool taekwondo class in her neighbourhood that charged almost nothing for enrolment, Serin didn't hesitate. It was one of the few happy moments in her life.

The master demonstrated the board break first, followed by some of the boys.

'Board breaking isn't about power,' the master stated. 'The most important thing is believing in yourself.'

He'd said the same thing about training the mind before the body so many times that Serin had got sick of it. But her eyes landed on one of the boys giving the demonstration, and her face turned bright red. She'd liked the boy for months. With a loud yell, the boy did multiple back kicks and broke one board after another. Serin applauded with the others until her palms hurt.

Afterwards, they came forward one at a time to try the kicks for themselves. No one was perfect, but everyone managed to break their boards, which all came pre-cracked to make it easier for the students.

Finally, Serin was up.

Can I do this?

The handsome boy who'd given the magnificent demonstration held up the board level with Serin's head. He gave her a small nod. Serin took a deep breath and got ready for her best move: the spinning back kick.

All eyes were on her.

Swallowing loud enough to hear, Serin spun. But she was so nervous that her foot swung through thin air. On her second try, she missed the board again and kicked the boy's hand instead, then fell on her backside for good measure.

Everyone was laughing. 'Hey now, anyone can make mistakes,' the master said, trying to settle them down, but it was all useless, because they wouldn't stop. Serin spent the rest of the lesson staring down at the floor, barely managed a nod as they closed for the day, and rushed out with her bag.

Although it was evening, it was still as bright as afternoon.

'Serin, you are a complete idiot,' she fumed, kicking innocent pebbles and dandelions. 'Might as well be a sea cucumber or a sea urchin for all the brains you have. Why can't I do anything right?'

Taekwondo was the one thing in Serin's life that she looked forward to. The only thing she could afford to dream about. It helped her get through the lonely hours at school, and it kept her awake in excitement as she pictured herself breaking boards at international demonstrations.

Finally, she kicked an empty can, which drew an arc in the air as it disappeared into the distance. Wishing she could have kicked the board half so well, Serin looked up and found herself in the alley outside her building.

Today, she spotted even more signs labelled *WE STAND AGAINST DEMOLITION* by the path. The neighbourhood was slated for redevelopment, which meant all the tenants had to leave the building, but the people there – like Serin and her mother – didn't have the money to find a new home. So the demolition plans kept getting pushed further and further back.

Recently, some of the neighbours had organized a demonstration, and when broadcasters arrived with TV cameras, the neighbours had shaved their heads as a show of protest. The thought that she might soon be driven out of her own home made Serin's steps even heavier.

She heard loud noises. The closer she got to the building, the louder they got. Someone was talking over a loudspeaker, and people were chanting, with the occasional swear word peppered between. Another protest, and it wasn't far from home.

There were two groups at the protest: one side wearing red headbands labelled *SAVE OUR HOMES*, and the other wearing black clothes and hats marked with matching logos. The two sides were pointing fingers and shouting and swearing, threatening to charge. Serin had seen it all before, but it had never been so intense.

A moment later, she heard sirens as police cruisers arrived on the scene. Not wanting to get involved, Serin quickly ducked into her unit.

She found her mother wearing reading glasses today, with some sewing in her hand.

'Welcome home, Serin. You must be hungry.'

In a corner of the room was a small table with a bowl of rice and a few scraps of sides. But Serin pretended not to see it. 'I don't feel like it,' she sighed, dropping her bag as if it were a boulder.

'Are you on one of those diets again?'

'No, I'm not. I want to sleep.'

Without even changing out of her clothes, Serin plunked down wearily on the blankets on the floor.

'Did something happen, honey?'

Serin didn't say a word. Her mother must not have been too curious, because she quickly went back to her sewing. It wasn't long before she put down one darned sock and reached for its holey twin. 'Mum,' Serin said, breaking her silence. 'Remember that nasty lady who used to live across the street? She—'

'Serin, be respectful to your elders.'

'But she *is* nasty,' Serin said. 'She says I should stop doing taekwondo, that it's totally useless. Do you think so too?'

Her mother replied, 'Nothing in this world is ever useless, Serin. It'll all come in handy someday.'

'You think I should just quit and spend more time studying? What am I good at, Mum?'

'You can do anything if you just put your mind to it,' her mother replied, struggling to thread her needle as the conversation seemed to be distracting her.

Serin turned in her blankets, pouting. 'I bet you don't even care. And can we please throw out those old things? Nobody *darns* clothes any more. It's not as if we can't afford new *socks*.'

'Just because we can afford them doesn't mean we should buy them.'

Her mother was always like this. Serin wished she would stop being so stubborn. That holey sock reminded Serin of herself. Old and frayed and miserable. She wished she could take the thing out of her mother's hands and toss it in the rubbish. For a moment Serin pretended to be asleep, but then she rose to her feet and pulled a thick book from the shelf.

'Say, Mum?' she asked, pausing dramatically. Her mother looked up over her reading glasses. 'If you could be born again, what kind of life would you want?'

'What is this, now?' her mother asked, perplexed, her hands still busy at work.

Serin sighed. 'Never mind,' she replied, and opened the book so her mother couldn't see what was inside. Her fingers flipped through the pages until they stopped at the same place as last time.

She stared down at her last hope, a Ticket to a future no one would believe.

The Ticket still shone brightly between the pages.

Episode 4
The First Night of the Rainy Season

Just before school closed for the summer, Serin finally got the news she was waiting for.

The radio forecasted rain.

But she couldn't tell her mother the truth. She spent the whole week before the start of the rainy season wondering how she should explain that she'd be away for days on end. She still hadn't thought of anything until the afternoon she had to leave – and so all she could do was leave a letter behind and rush out the door:

I'll be staying with a friend for a few days.

It was an obvious lie because Serin had never told her mother she had any friends. But what did it matter? By this time next week, she could have the best life in the entire world and never have to come back here again.

Putting on her trainers, which never looked new no matter how much she washed them, Serin went into town, at the centre of which was the railway station.

It had been a long time since she'd gone to town, and even longer since she'd last taken a train. She'd been in primary school, holding her mother's hand, back then.

The train bound for Rainbow Town is now approaching. Please remain behind the safety line and mind the gap.

Serin had never paid much attention to the station, but because it was a Friday and the evening rush hour, the platforms were packed. She got lost near the platform gates and almost missed the train right in front of her. But fortunately, she managed to slip inside just as the doors shut.

It was only after scrambling into a seat that it finally hit her: she had left home.

So far so good, she thought, eyes scanning her surroundings.

A young man who seemed to be a year or two her senior with earphones in his ears was watching something on his laptop – a movie or a show, she couldn't tell. His half-open bag seemed to be stuffed with textbooks. She didn't mean to snoop, but Serin spotted the name of a school on the spines. It was a famous university, so prestigious that secondary schools put up congratulatory signs each year for graduates who were accepted there. The university that all the clever students wanted to enter.

If only, thought Serin. When she was little, she'd wanted to aim for that school too, but as she grew, she'd realized that it was simply too far out of reach.

The man couldn't have been much older than her, but he lived in a totally different world. Serin couldn't help but steal glances in his direction throughout the train ride, until he looked up and met her gaze. She turned red with embarrassment and fixed her eyes on the window instead.

It was getting darker outside, and not just because of sunset. Dark clouds were pushing into the sky. And the trees – even the biggest, tallest ones – were shaking and shivering, almost dancing in the wind.

Serin pulled out her invitation and Ticket and read through their contents one more time.

The invitation hadn't set a date, simply stating she was to visit on the first day of the rainy season.

Can these Dokkaebi really change my life?
And if they can, what kind of life do I want?

One question followed another, none of them with easy answers. Serin closed her eyes and let herself sink into the seat, bumpy ride and all. Her head felt heavy.

When she woke up, the world outside was darker than before, and the wind stronger.

Then there was an announcement:

'We will soon arrive at Rainbow Town. This is the train's final destination, and all passengers must disembark. Passengers are reminded to take all their belongings when they exit the train.'

Serin picked up her orange umbrella. She was ready to disembark.

When the train stopped and the doors opened, the passengers rose in unison and made their way to the doors. The deafening silence quickly gave way to a small clamour.

Serin waited until everyone else had gone before stepping on to the platform.

Instantly, a cool breeze caressed her face. It felt like a gentle welcome. The wind was full of moisture, which meant the weather forecast was right and rain would start within the day. Serin haphazardly patted down her wind-tangled hair and looked around.

Rainbow Town wasn't as large as she'd expected. It was mostly low-rise buildings, maybe because they were near a train station. There were no rice paddies around, which meant it wasn't exactly a rural village, but this was definitely no metropolis.

Taking a deep breath, Serin pulled out a rough, hand-drawn map and left the station.

Taxi drivers huddled in small groups outside the station, cigarettes in hand. They looked at Serin as though wondering if she needed a taxi, but she quickly looked away. The train Ticket had cost almost her entire savings.

Fortunately, she had two strong legs from years of climbing

up and down a steep hillside. But just to make certain the drivers didn't get the wrong idea, she strode briskly away.

The smooth pavement soon gave way to dirt. Serin started to doubt the badly drawn map in her hand as she walked along something that barely counted as a road.

But on and on she went, until she reached a little village scarcely big enough for a dozen families. An old street lamp lit the village entrance, but no one was outside.

Under the lamp, Serin checked the address on her map once more. If she had copied it down correctly, the abandoned house was somewhere in this village. Her legs were starting to ache. Serin massaged her knees, wanting nothing more than to sit down somewhere – anywhere – for some rest, but she had to find the house before it went completely dark.

'Not here, either,' Serin was forced to admit, after checking the buildings one by one. There was just one house left.

Suddenly, there was a noise. A faint commotion. With an ominous feeling, Serin rushed over to the scene.

There was a run-down house, and in front of it, an elderly man on the ground. He was surrounded by three men in their mid-twenties to early thirties, and it was clear from the way they stood that they were not there for a friendly chat.

'And all you had to do was be nice and hand over the Ticket like a good old man,' said one of the young men. He wore a sleeveless yellow shirt, topped with bleach-blond hair, and had a golden chain around his neck. 'We just want to see one of those famous Dokkaebi Tickets, what's the harm here? Just one peek, old man, we're good boys.'

The elderly man was unyielding. 'Don't you dare!' he scolded from the ground. 'I know what you're up to, you thugs. Shaking down hapless pedestrians instead of looking for jobs, you make me sick!'

'Did you call us thugs, old man? You're hurting our feelings,' said another one of the men, who looked mean enough to give a real Dokkaebi a run for his money. He leaned in closer to the elder. 'It's just one look. Did you want us to say the magic word, too?'

'I'm not going to fall for that,' the elderly man said, snorting, and slowly rose to his feet, shaking dirt off his hands. He was small in stature, but didn't seem intimidated at all by the threatening men. 'I've no Ticket to show you thugs, and even if I did, you don't deserve to see it!' he said defiantly, glaring hard enough to shoot lasers out of his eyes.

The young men burst into laughter.

One of them, who wore a leather jacket with an eagle pattern on the back, stepped forward, hauling a baseball bat off his shoulder. He seemed to be the leader of the gang.

'We asked you nicely, old man. You brought this on yourself, got that?'

The blond man tilted his head harshly from side to side, making a threatening crack. The mean-looking one brandished his fists.

Instantly, the elderly man shrank. His bravado gone, he wrapped his head in his hands and screamed.

The young men snickered. 'Hah! We haven't even started, old man – at least try to put up a good fight,' said the leader. He gave a snide grin and stepped forward.

At least, he tried to. Without warning, something pulled him up by the scruff of his black leather jacket.

'Hey! What is this?' the man demanded, but he couldn't see anything. 'Let me go!' he cried. Though he put up a comical struggle, his jacket stayed up in the air, only rising higher and higher until the man was more than his own height off the ground. Then he was flung into the darkened woods.

The elderly man was on the ground, while the other thugs

stood frozen with their eyes locked in the direction their leader had flown. Slowly, they turned to exchange glances, which was precisely when one of them also rose into the air, perhaps half a foot this time, and was flung into the woods as though struck by a car.

The blond one was all alone now. Realizing that something was going horribly wrong, he scrambled desperately into the woods himself – whether to get his friends or to run away, Serin couldn't tell – running as fast as his legs could carry him.

But a second later, there was a *thud*, and the sound of someone rolling across the ground. The elderly man tentatively peered up. Then he flinched and flung himself backwards as though he himself had been thrown.

'G-get away from me!'

Standing before him was something Serin could never have imagined in a million years. But she and the elderly man knew exactly what – or who – this was. There was no other word to describe the towering figure, human but not quite. The elderly man rubbed his eyes again and again.

A Dokkaebi.

A sudden rain shower began, summoning a refreshing melody of water against the foliage.

Episode 5

The Gatekeeper

Serin was just as shocked as the elderly man.

The sudden rain soaked her completely, hair and clothes and all, but she didn't even think about opening her umbrella.

The Dokkaebi looked like a large person, but with longer arms and shorter legs – almost like a gorilla – and he had emerged from the abandoned house and tossed aside the thugs in the blink of an eye. And in the end, he had even picked up the baseball bat and batted away the fleeing man.

Serin finally recalled what she'd read in the book: Dokkaebi were guides to the Rainfall Market, and were thus invisible to people who hadn't been invited. From the stupid looks on the thugs' faces, the author must have been telling the truth.

Before Serin knew it, the Dokkaebi had turned from the elderly man to her, peering out from behind a nearby building. She finally got a close look at his face.

Other than the small horn rising from the top of his head, the Dokkaebi looked almost human. But he was tall enough to give a basketball player a run for his money.

Without a word, the Dokkaebi looked from Serin to the elderly man, then to Serin again, and gestured for them to follow. He then disappeared into the abandoned house. The rain only grew worse.

Serin opened her umbrella and rushed to the elderly man's side. 'Sir, are you all right?'

The elderly man, whose jaw had dropped enough to collect a mouthful of rain, flinched once more. 'Who are you?'

'My name is Serin. I have a Ticket too, so I came to visit the Rainfall Market. Are you hurt?' She took the elderly man's arm.

He allowed her to help him rise, and still leaning on her for support, stood up properly. The elderly man seemed to have been more frightened by the Dokkaebi than the young men. Serin could relate. Her knees had been knocking the whole time, and she'd been standing a fair distance away.

'Thank you, young lady. I-I never thought I'd see a real Dokkaebi in the flesh.'

The elderly man opened up his own umbrella. Even Serin could tell it was an expensive model. And when he dusted himself off and put on his posh top hat, he looked like a completely new man. He couldn't have been younger than sixty-five, but now that he was no longer cowering in fear, he looked as healthy as a man half his age, and walked like one too.

'Let's go on in, now,' he said gently, leading the way. Serin followed the elderly man up the stairs to the wide-open door.

Somewhere inside the house was a dim light.

As if he'd done all this before, the elderly man marched easily across the threshold. Serin paused and took a deep breath. She was ready.

They vanished into the house, and once again the street was utterly silent.

Serin couldn't believe her eyes. She was sure she'd walked into a dilapidated building, but beyond the door was a vast, sprawling field of flowers. And the sun was shining high in the sky. She and the elderly man exchanged quizzical glances, but quickly went on their way.

Just ten paces ahead stood the Dokkaebi from before. At some point, a triangular yellow flag had appeared in his hand, the kind tour guides used to lead sightseers through crowded attractions. Serin and the elderly man went up to the Dokkaebi, following a small trail in the field.

In the shadows, the Dokkaebi had been a terror. But now, as the sun shone down, Serin could see that while the Dokkaebi was large, he had a surprisingly gentle face. He waited patiently for her and the man to snap out of their daze and follow him.

From up close, the Dokkaebi looked even more endearing. He was shirtless, but wore a pair of blue overalls with only one side secured on his shoulder, almost like a little child. Over his breast was a tiny butterfly-shaped nametag, with the name 'Toriya' drawn across it in a crooked hand.

'"Toriya?"' Serin said out loud, and the Dokkaebi nodded. That was his name. He pointed at Serin.

'Me?' she replied. 'My name is Serin.'

'Se . . . rin . . .' the Dokkaebi pronounced with some difficulty.

Beaming, Serin replied, 'That's right. So is this the Rainfall Market?'

'Market,' Toriya uttered, pointing at a white building in the distance.

Beyond the field of flowers stood what looked like a castle, or maybe a tower. Scattered around the long, thin structure were small houses, the kind that seemed to have come straight out of a fairy tale.

'Wow,' Serin gasped. 'If I go there, can I really get a new life?'

Toriya did not respond. He simply scratched his head with one long, sharp claw. He did not seem to be used to human language. Meanwhile, the elderly man stood two paces away as Serin peppered Toriya with questions.

'It's okay,' Serin said reassuringly. 'Sir, I don't think Toriya means to hurt us.'

But the elderly man remained petrified behind her.

Toriya did not spare him a glance as he turned around and headed for the Rainfall Market. He was so tall that for each step he took, Serin and the elderly man had to take two or three to keep pace. But it wasn't so hard, because Toriya was a slow walker – whether he was always that way or slowing down for their sake, Serin didn't know.

Suddenly, Toriya froze. He swerved, taking a long detour around the path through the flowers. Serin watched him in confusion, before going up to the spot where Toriya had turned.

She'd expected to see something dangerous, like a large snake. But all she found on the well-trodden road were some pebbles. Assuming that Toriya had seen something she had not, she glanced down.

A caterpillar wriggled across the road before her feet.

Really? A caterpillar? Serin wondered.

But just as Serin caught up to him, Toriya stopped again.

This time, he squatted on the road and stared for what seemed like forever at something on the ground: a beautiful purple flower in full bloom. Toriya was so focused on the flower that Serin couldn't bring herself to interrupt him.

So she looked into his eyes.

Toriya almost appeared to be in love with the flower, like he wanted to take it with him.

Serin knelt down and picked the flower for him, and Toriya cheered like a little child. She wondered if they would reach the Market before the rainy season ended. But fortunately, Toriya did not stop on the way again. He must not have spotted any scary bugs or pretty flowers.

*

The Rainfall Market's main building looked like a large stack of marshmallows arranged like a tower. It was so much taller and more majestic than the rest of the buildings, that Serin supposed if she stood at the very top, everything on the ground would look like matchboxes. The entrance was so large that Toriya would not have to duck when they walked inside.

The doors slid open on their own almost like a haunted house. But immediately, Serin's ears were assaulted by deafening music. A party was well under way.

Serin briefly wondered if Toriya had accidentally led her to a club. The elderly man, too, cleared his throat in discomfort. A disco ball spun rapidly overhead, and all they could see inside were the vague outlines of moving people.

Dokkaebi dressed for a rave performed music on a stage as tall as Serin, while male Dokkaebi dressed in impeccable waiters' suits came up and offered them drinks on a platter. Serin wasn't sure she wanted any, but the elderly man took two glasses and held one out to her. Serin had to accept.

'Huh?'

She'd assumed the drink was alcoholic, but it was actually fruit juice. She couldn't tell what the fruit was, but it was so sweet and cool that if she saw the waiter again, she would ask for another glass even if it meant sounding like a glutton. The elderly man also closed his eyes as he enjoyed the delectable drink, singing its praises.

It was not long before the party wound down. Serin and the elderly man must have been the last guests to arrive, because the doors behind them were shut and barred.

THUD.

The doors closed as loudly as they had been silent when they opened. The Dokkaebi on the stage, who had been singing and dancing until their clothes were soaked in sweat, took their bows as they left the stage to a flurry of applause. With the music gone, the Rainfall Market was as quiet as a library.

The curtains fell. A lone Dokkaebi stepped forward on to the stage.

Dressed in an immaculate purple suit and an eye-catching yellow tie, the Dokkaebi was stylish even by human standards. His hair was lathered with pomade and combed all the way over to one side, and he sported a handsome moustache. The Dokkaebi made such a powerful impression that no one would forget how he looked.

Taking the microphone, the Dokkaebi spoke:

'Esteemed guests! My name is Durof, and it is my pleasure to welcome you today,' he said, and after a moment's pause, continued dramatically:

'Welcome, one and all! Welcome to the Rainfall Market!'

Episode 6

The Rainfall Market

Excited murmurs filled the hall when Durof took the stage. Soon, the lights grew brighter and brighter until they lit up the entire venue. Easily a hundred people crowded the hall, some looking terrified while others had their arms crossed confidently.

Serin's eyes flew in every direction as she took in the Rainfall Market, the people, and more. But the most captivating person in the room was, of course, the Dokkaebi in the spotlight.

'Thank you for making the journey to the Rainfall Market,' Durof continued, warmly making eye contact with the people gathered closest to the stage. 'I understand that you all have questions – questions that deserve answers – but I would first like to give a brief introduction.' Durof loosened his tie slightly. 'The Rainfall Market boasts a long and storied tradition. As the greatest market in the world, we invite humans each year to make use of our services – all thanks to our beloved leader and chief, whose love for humankind knows no bounds. In accordance with his will, we vow to do all we can to make your stay with us a comfortable one.'

Durof placed his right hand over his heart and gave a deep bow.

'Now that the formalities are done with,' he said and snapped his fingers, signalling a beautiful female Dokkaebi to come forward with a platter covered in cloth. 'Let us proceed to the main event.'

As the beautiful Dokkaebi set the platter on the table Durof went on: 'The moment you've all been waiting for!

'Sick of your misery and misfortune? Sick of doing nothing but dream of the life you desire? Well, no more! Because we can make your dreams a reality!'

He paused dramatically, and continued:

'Allow me to present the pride and joy of the Rainfall Market: the Dokkaebi Orbs!'

Durof pulled the cloth off the platter with an elegant flourish that must have taken half a day to master. The cloth went taut in midair and fluttered to the back of the stage.

The crowd gasped, eyes locked on the objects on the platter. Serin had to stand on tiptoes and squint to make out anything at all from the back of the hall. The elderly man craned his neck as well.

Shining orbs gleamed on the platter like jewels – some the size of ping pong balls, others large enough to bowl with. Durof picked one up. 'What do you think? Beautiful, don't you agree? Each of these fine Dokkaebi Orbs contains the extraordinary – or ordinary – life you desire!'

A brave hand rose into the air. 'How much?'

'It is not human currency we seek,' Durof replied. 'Each store in the Rainfall Market has one Orb for purchase. Simply take the gold coins we pay you in exchange for your misfortune, spend it at the establishment, and the Orb will be yours. No extra charge!'

The hall erupted into cheers and applause. A satisfied grin rose to Durof's lips, his moustache almost rising to his ears. 'Our stores are home to countless Dokkaebi Orbs, which we have collected over the years,' he continued. 'Please take your time and browse our offerings, and make your choice before the end of the rainy season.'

The man who had raised his hand earlier asked, 'What if

we don't choose by then?' Serin looked at him closely this time. He wore angular horn-rimmed glasses and held a notepad and pen, the kind of person who must have been the teacher's pet at school.

Appropriately, Durof took on the bearing of a teacher as he replied, 'Excellent question. If you do not choose a Dokkaebi Orb at all, nothing will happen. You may choose to leave the Rainfall Market at any time, with or without a Dokkaebi Orb. However, there is something very important that you all must keep in mind,' he said, picking up a steaming cup of tea from the table and gulping it down in one go without even flinching. 'If you should fail to *leave* the Rainfall Market before the end of the rainy season,' he said, turning his cup to show the audience that he had emptied it completely, 'those of you still here on our premises will vanish for all time.'

It was like someone had splashed cold water over them all. Durof noted his audience's shock and gave an exaggerated laugh, filling the silence. 'Not to worry, my esteemed guests! You have plenty of time to make your choice and depart,' he assured them. 'The rainy season has only just begun, and is scheduled to last for one week, nine hours, forty-four minutes and thirty-two seconds. For more details, please refer to our clock, set to Dokkaebi Standard Time.' Durof pointed at the entrance. The clock hung over the door. It had no hands, because it was a massive hourglass filled with water. A single droplet fell into the lower half.

'As for how you might use your Dokkaebi Orbs,' Durof said, 'the details will be provided at the Misfortune Pawnshop, which you will visit next. We've also prepared guidebooks for your reference.'

He gave the beautiful Dokkaebi a look. She nodded and brought out a stack of small guidebooks.

The crowds surged, everyone pushing and shoving to get a copy first. Some people seemed more interested in the beautiful assistant than the handbook, taking more time than the others. Serin and the elderly man, however, waited their turn patiently and took the last two copies.

The guidebook was small and thin, and looked much like the kind offered at tourist attractions. It could be folded up and carried around with ease, and the cover, coated to be waterproof, bore the words *A Guide to the Rainfall Market* in large letters.

Serin couldn't wait. She peeled open her guidebook.

*We hereby ask all customers to take note of the following rules.
1. The gold coins from the Misfortune Pawnshop may only be spent within the Rainfall Market.
2. The gold coins from the Misfortune Pawnshop are only valid during that year's rainy season.
3. Once a Dokkaebi Orb has been taken to the human world, it may not be refunded or exchanged.
4. The happiness within a Dokkaebi Orb may be unleashed at the holder's convenience with a specific incantation.
5. A Dokkaebi Orb that has been abandoned or surrendered will return to its original owner.

The rest of the pages included more tips, smaller maps showing the locations of the stores, and recommended routes for navigating the Rainfall Market. The restaurant recommendation section highlighted an eatery run by the brothers Bordo and Bormo, complete with a picture of two identical smiling Dokkaebi.

The final page of the guidebook even included a discount

coupon for the Casino. Serin didn't have any business there, but decided to keep the coupon just in case.

'Well, well, would you look at the time?' Durof said dramatically. 'Esteemed guests, I do believe the hour is growing late. But before you turn in for the evening at the accommodations we have prepared, please make your way to the Pawnshop to trade in your misfortune. Our gatekeeper Toriya will show you the way.'

Durof pointed a finger at the door on the opposite side of the entrance, where stood Toriya – still holding the childish yellow flag.

'And with that, I bid you all good evening,' said Durof. 'If you have any questions or seek a specific Dokkaebi Orb, please do not hesitate to speak to yours truly at the Information Desk,' he said with one final courteous bow.

Slowly, the crowds made their way to Toriya. He did not lead the group to the Pawnshop immediately, however. There was one last thing for him to check: the Tickets. Toriya examined each Ticket, stamped it, and handed a wristwatch to the holder of the verified Ticket.

The watch was a miniature version of the hourglass hanging on the wall, and strangely, no matter which way it was held up, the water only ever flowed in one direction.

Even more strangely, everyone else's Tickets were silver. Serin froze, wondering if there had been a mistake, but Toriya took one look at her gold Ticket and stamped it loudly.

Durof twitched from the stage.

But no one, not even Serin, noticed. With a sigh of relief, she went up to the elderly man. He had got his Ticket stamped before her.

Having checked the Tickets and handed out the watches, Toriya led the crowd down a set of stairs. Unlike the main entrance, the staircase was so narrow that he had to hunch as he walked. A long line of people followed.

It did not take too long, however, for the crowds to disappear down the stairs. The sound of voices faded, as did their footsteps.

The hall was silent once more, as if no one had ever been there.

Episode 7
The Misfortune Pawnshop

Bulbs of incandescent light hung low from the ceiling. Not only were they dim, they even flickered on and off sometimes, as if about to expire. And the ceiling was so low that Toriya, though curled as tight as possible for someone of his stature, kept hitting his head. Each time Serin heard a thud, clumps of dirt fell before her. Some people clung to their neighbours in fright, and apologized. And then there were the people who already seemed eager to argue.

'Stop pushing!'

'Hurry it up.'

To make matters worse, the stairs going down were so steep that one wrong step could send them falling. The further they descended, the more humid it became – and worse yet, the smell of mould assaulted their nostrils. This was no place for a long stay.

'How much deeper do we have to go?' someone complained. But Toriya pushed stubbornly onward, as though he could not hear a thing.

Suddenly, a man at the very front lost his footing, falling forward. But there was no sound of people rolling down the stairs – they had reached the very bottom, and the crowd seemed more concerned about the Pawnshop than the fallen man.

A slight distance from the bottom of the steps was a ramshackle building, the kind that might pass for a faded country corner store, dusty merchandise and all. But from up close, it looked completely different.

What in the world is this place?

The Pawnshop must have been hiding *something* important, because an entire wall was blocked off by a combination of iron bars and a thick glass pane. The middle of the glass pane was dotted with a cluster of small holes, and directly below those holes was one large hole big enough to fit a person's head.

The crowd slowly made their way to the building, but then froze.

Lounging behind the glass pane was a Dokkaebi, pipe held between grumpy lips. The building was dense with smoke from the pipe, almost enough to pass for a house on fire.

This Dokkaebi had a ferocious bearing and wore thick makeup and a bun of curly hair along with shiny golden jewellery, including hoop earrings that reminded Serin of the hanging handles on public buses. Shiny rings decorated each of the Dokkaebi's fingers, too. But what stood out more than anything was the Dokkaebi's necklace – or more accurately, bundle of necklaces. Golden chains with links the size of a baby's fists. It was a wonder the Dokkaebi could sit up at all.

Serin quickly consulted her guidebook. Luckily, she found the Dokkaebi she was looking for on the second page.

Berna. The woman who owned the Misfortune Pawnshop. In the guidebook, she was pictured smoking a pipe, with the distinct look of someone who had no interest in anything at all.

Berna looked up, and spotting the long line of humans, picked up a wired microphone.

'All of you—' she began, but realizing that the microphone was silent, took her other hand from under her chin and tapped on the microphone.

Everyone winced as the speakers screamed. With an irritated sigh, Berna tossed the microphone to the floor.

With all eyes on her, Berna took a deep breath and boomed loud enough for even Serin to hear from the back:

'Let's skip the pleasantries. I hate repeating myself, so if you get distracted now and waste my time later, I am going to pull down your trousers and kick your backside out of my pawnshop. Understood?'

As Berna's voice echoed off the cavernous walls, a man snickered, shoulders bouncing. He must have assumed that Berna was joking. But he quickly realized that no one else was laughing. There was an awkward silence as the crowd held their breath, waiting for Berna to follow up on her threat.

Fortunately she simply stared daggers at the man before continuing.

'In a moment, my dear Toriya will hand out blank Dokkaebi Orbs to each of you. Once you have your Orb, hold it in both hands and think of the things in life you wish would disappear, and recite these words – *druu epp zulaa*. Repeat after me. *Druu epp zulaa.*'

Like a choir, the crowd repeated the spell in unison. Those who didn't hear it chose to ask their neighbours rather than risk Berna's wrath.

'Keep on practising until you've filled up your Dokkaebi Orb. And don't disturb the others.' Then she added as an afterthought, 'The most important thing about a Dokkaebi Orb is its shine. One spot of dirt means one less gold coin for you.'

Now it was Toriya's turn. He pulled out one Dokkaebi Orb after another from the front pocket of his overalls, which was seemingly bottomless from the way he kept on bringing them up. Though they looked to be the size of peas in Toriya's hand, in Serin's they were as big as melons.

Unlike the ones Durof had shown on stage, the Orbs the

customers received were perfectly clear, with no colour at all. Dozens, maybe more than a hundred Orbs shone faintly in the dim cavern.

Then, Serin heard the incantation all around her. People reciting it softly. So she closed her eyes and thought slowly back to her own misfortune. It was not hard at all.

Ever since her father passed away, her family had been poor.

Serin's mother was too busy to pay her any attention, and her younger sister Yerin ran away from home last year and never contacted them again.

Serin had no friends, and no one who encouraged her and believed in her.

She didn't ask for much.

All she wanted was an ordinary life.

Parents who would be there at graduation.

A sister to share all her secrets with, like a best friend.

But Serin was always alone. Always lonely.

The hard times flashed before her eyes.

Suddenly, it occurred to Serin that she might have been thinking for too long. She opened her eyes.

A few people were still reciting the spell, but most were crowded near the Pawnshop counter or chatting with their neighbours. One impatient customer had already gone to Berna for an appraisal. Beyond the glass, the smoke had got so thick that Serin could only just make out Berna's face. Once more, Serin closed her eyes and filled her Dokkaebi Orb with her misfortune, which meant she ended up at the back of the queue again.

'Hm . . .' Berna intoned, looking over each Orb with the focus of a surgeon.

She weighed the Orbs on a scale and scrutinized them with

a jeweller's loupe before finally reaching into a large sack and dispensing a handful of gold coins. At first glance, it looked like the amount was random, but Serin realized that sometimes, Berna would take back one or two coins or add a few more. Surprisingly, she had a system of sorts.

That reminded Serin of something Berna had said earlier. *Oh, right!* She looked around and found others who must have had the same thought, because they were studying their Dokkaebi Orbs from every angle, misting and polishing them on their sleeves.

Serin, too, pulled out her handkerchief and polished and polished and polished. She had never liked the quaint flower-print handkerchief, but her mother had insisted that she carry one around at all times, just in case.

Before she knew it, the line had got shorter, then disappeared. Serin was still polishing away when Berna impatiently snatched up the Orb, handkerchief and all.

'Er, I—' Serin began, but stopped. Berna was not one to stand for interruption, she realized.

Berna held Serin's Dokkaebi Orb up to the fluorescent light, tapped away on a calculator, then handed over so many gold coins that Serin could barely hold them all. Then Berna wrapped up the Orb in Serin's handkerchief and placed it on the same shelf as the rest of the Orbs.

Then she gave Serin a look that said her business was finished and Serin found herself rushing away in fright.

With a long, deep, and smoky sigh, Berna watched Serin depart – eyes intent on the Ticket sticking out of her pocket. Once the pawnshop was empty, she pulled out a radio.

'That's correct. I've just found the human with the Golden Ticket.'

A voice on the other end gave her a command. Berna pulled a small jewellery box from the desk and opened it. In a puff of smoke, an ink-black shadow emerged. The shadow circled her briefly before stopping on top of the desk.

'Follow the human girl who just left. The one with the Golden Ticket. This is her scent,' Berna said, coaxing the shadow to smell Serin's handkerchief. The shadow took on a monstrous form, sniffed, then turned into a cloud of smoke and glided away.

Then the ink-black shadow faded into the darkness.

Running a metal nail file over her already-immaculate nails, Berna whispered, 'I won't let you have your way, mark my words.'

Because Serin was the last to hand over her Dokkaebi Orb, she trailed behind the other customers as they filtered out of the caverns. But then she noticed that her shoelaces were untied. She bent down and worked at the knots for a minute, then looked back up.

Everyone else was gone.

Serin walked on rapidly, hoping to catch up to the others, but she quickly realized she was lost. The dark cavern looked even darker now, and she couldn't tell which direction she'd come from.

She yelled at the top of her lungs, 'Is anyone there?', but only her own echoing voice answered the call. Serin wondered if she should try turning around to go back to the Pawnshop, but noticed a small, flaming torch in the distance. It almost seemed to be floating, precisely at eye-level, and gave Serin goosebumps. But she was more scared of the dark than the mysterious flame, so she drew near without much thought.

Where in the world am I?

Upon closer inspection, the torch was secured to the wall with a metal ring. Next to it was an unmarked, rusted metal door. No one guarded it, but from the look of the lock, it was clear that visitors were not welcome. Serin tried pushing the door, but it refused to budge. Finally, she spotted a sign marked with a red 'X'. The room was clearly off-limits.

Serin sighed and turned around.

'There you are,' a familiar voice said from overhead.

She looked up and found Durof the moustached Dokkaebi, leaning so close it was uncomfortable.

'This would be the dungeon entrance,' Durof explained before Serin could catch her breath.

'Th-the dungeon?' Serin repeated. She'd thought the Rainfall Market was strange, but she'd never imagined there might be a prison here.

'A terrible place,' said Durof, shuddering. 'The poor souls who enter rarely see the light of day again.'

Serin gulped, then realized she should ask, 'What are you doing here?'

'Ah! Where are my manners? How unbecoming of me to speak to a lady without even explaining myself.' He tapped his forehead, careful not to touch his immaculate hairstyle. 'Miss, you are a very special customer. One of a rare few who arrive at our doorstep with an unusual kind of Ticket, which entitles you to additional benefits.'

'M-me?' Serin asked, reaching into her pocket to make sure her Ticket was still there.

Durof pulled a teacup seemingly out of thin air, took a sip, and replied, 'Indeed. Miss, might I examine your Ticket for a moment?'

Slowly, carefully, Serin pulled out the Ticket and held it out for Durof. He pulled on the pair of reading glasses he wore around his neck and studied the Ticket, his nose almost touching the golden surface.

'This is indeed a Golden Ticket,' he said with a whistle.

Not knowing what a Golden Ticket meant for her, Serin waited for him to continue.

'Miss,' Durof said, 'might I ask you to accompany me to the Information Desk? We have many things to discuss, and all of it is bound to please you.'

Already pleased at the prospect of escaping the caverns, Serin nodded.

'Right this way, Miss.'

Durof led the way, and Serin followed as they quickly disappeared into the darkness.

Episode 8
The Information Desk

The Information Desk was not far from the Rainfall Market entrance. Unlike the caverns, it was brightly lit – so much so that it took Serin's eyes a moment to adjust.

Durof turned a shiny metal doorknob. 'Please, after you.'

The first thing Serin saw was a marble floor polished to a mirror sheen. Almost all of that marble floor was covered by luxurious sofas, leaving only a sliver as a corridor. But Serin didn't see anyone else. The other customers, she guessed, must have gone to the accommodations Durof mentioned earlier.

Then she spotted a young Dokkaebi man in blue overalls hard at work in a corner, trying to adjust the angle of a sofa. He was so focused on his work that he didn't notice the new arrivals until Durof loudly cleared his throat.

'Mr Durof!' the Dokkaebi squawked, jumping to his feet and knocking the sofa back to its slant.

Durof simply raised a hand in greeting.

The floor was so clean Serin could probably eat off it. Did they polish it every day, or had the Dokkaebi only cleaned up for the grand opening? The pristine white wallpaper and the white furniture even reminded her of a hospital. Serin tried to walk as lightly as possible so she wouldn't track dirt on to the floor, but the Dokkaebi in overalls was already rushing over with a look of horror on his face. He trailed after her with a mop, sweeping away behind her like in a backwards curling match.

Serin opened her mouth to apologize, but Durof spoke first.

'And this here is my workstation. The Information Desk.'

Serin turned. The desk was just as white as the rest of the room, and on top was a blindingly shiny mother-of-pearl nameplate with *DUROF* written on the front. On either side stood sculptures of all sorts, arranged by size.

'Please, do take a seat,' Durof insisted, gesturing at the office chair in front of the desk. He went around behind the desk and sat in a chair that reminded Serin distinctly of a throne. 'Coffee?' he asked, picking up two packs of instant coffee.

'N-no thank you.'

Durof did not ask twice. He put down one of the packs, emptied the other into a cup, and poured boiling water from a kettle Serin had taken for a humidifier. A fragrant aroma filled the room.

'Allow me to explain why I invited you here,' Durof said, pushing aside a towering stack of documents. They seemed to be letters sent from the human world. 'Miss, I wish to explain the sheer magnitude of your good fortune in obtaining that Ticket. Might I be so bold as to ask for your name?'

Serin was scrutinizing the pile of letters out of the corner of her eye, trying to see if she could spot her own. 'It's Serin. Kim Serin,' she said.

Durof took a sip of coffee. 'It is a pleasure to make your acquaintance, Miss Serin. As I explained earlier, your Ticket is highly unusual, as you might have surmised from its colour. A Golden Ticket.'

Once more, Serin looked down at the Ticket. Somehow it looked even more important than before.

'The holder of a Golden Ticket is entitled to possess multiple Dokkaebi Orbs, and is even allowed to peer into each

Orb to closely examine the life it offers. A sort of second-hand experience, if you will. And unlike our other customers, who must seek out these Orbs on their own, VIPs need only ask for the Orb they desire, and they will be borne away to the shops of their choice by one of our complimentary spirit creatures.'

Durof rose and ran a hand over one of the statues displayed on either side of his nameplate. Serin had never been overseas, but she imagined she might find such souvenirs while on holiday in a foreign country.

'Now let me see . . . which will it be?'

Rubbing the palms of his hands, Durof examined the statues on his desk one by one, as giddy as a boy in a candy store.

Finally, his gaze fell on the statue at the very end. It was shaped like a cat.

'Aha,' he said. 'This should do.' Durof picked up the statue and recited what sounded like a magic spell.

What came next was straight out of Serin's wildest dreams.

The statue on the desk trembled, cracks appearing on its surface, and in the blink of an eye, the stone cat was a furry one. The cat shook off the dust and leapt on Durof, licking his face until it was slick with saliva.

With great difficulty, Durof calmed the cat, pulled it off his face, and placed it on the desk.

'His name is Issha,' Durof explained. 'He hasn't stretched his legs in quite some—'

Before Durof could finish, Issha began prodding at the other statues, pushing them off the desk one by one. Fortunately, Durof managed to catch them all before they hit the ground. Straightening himself while desperately trying to restore the hairstyle Issha had ruined, he added, 'Issha here is a spirit creature, a special bonus for Golden Ticket holders. He may appear to be an ordinary cat, but he possesses unusual powers.' He pulled up Issha by the scruff of his neck before the cat could chew through the rest of his backrest. 'You could carry him around in your pocket, like so,' Durof said, placing Issha into his jacket pocket. Suddenly, Issha was so tiny that only his head was visible. Then Durof pulled Issha out and tossed him into the air.

Horrified, Serin snapped out of her reverie and reached out to catch Issha. But he was much too far away. Issha rose into the air, then began to fall, completely oblivious.

'No!' Serin screamed, shutting her eyes.

There was a moment of silence. Hoping against hope that the little cat had landed on his paws, or at least wasn't badly hurt, she let herself open one eye, only very slightly.

Both her eyes flew open.

Where she'd expected a small cat, she found a fat feline the size of a refrigerator. His eyes were lazily narrowed, looking down on both Serin and Durof, all hints of innocence replaced by condescension.

'No need to worry on his account,' Durof assured her. 'The higher the height he falls from, the larger he will get.' Then he clapped twice, and the cat slowly got to his feet and waddled to their side. 'He will even carry you to your destination,' he said with all the charm of a salesman, and sat atop Issha's back with one leg elegantly crossed over the other. Then he climbed off and gave Issha's tail a tug. The cat shrank again.

Serin could scarcely pick up her jaw off the floor.

Issha the kitten disappeared somewhere behind Durof's desk, then returned with what looked like a tiny fishing pole in his mouth, pushing the pole into Durof's hand. He took the toy and began to shake the end for Issha's amusement.

'He has a very sensitive nose,' Durof went on. 'Perfect for navigation, although he can be easily distracted by food, the gluttonous creature. Issha even understands speech. Simply tell him which Dokkaebi Orb you want, or the name of a Dokkaebi you wish to see, and he will take you there.'

Durof put his hands under Issha's front legs and held him up for Serin. Issha met her gaze with eyes so shiny and innocent that she nearly melted.

'And last, but certainly not least,' said Durof, taking out a light green Dokkaebi Orb and placing it in Issha's mouth.

Issha's eyes glowed green and shot beams of light at Serin, projecting dreamlike images before her. But before the images could get clearer, the light disappeared. The Dokkaebi Orb was in Durof's hand once more.

'No need for alarm, that was simply a demonstration,' he said. 'We – Dokkaebi and Issha here – have the power to look into Dokkaebi Orbs as we please. And to show their contents to holders of the Golden Ticket.' Taking out a comb the size of a hatchet from his back pocket, he swept back his hair. 'It will only be a short preview, of course, but it should be of great assistance as you choose which Dokkaebi Orb you wish to take to the human world.'

The green Dokkaebi Orb shone as brightly as the mother-of-pearl nameplate on Durof's desk, but Serin was more interested in Issha. He was staring directly at her.

'I hope these benefits please you, Miss Serin,' Durof said confidently.

Serin replied, 'Yes, thank you. But are you sure I can keep this cat?'

'For the duration of your stay at the Rainfall Market, Issha is yours,' Durof said, handing the cat to Serin.

The second Issha was placed in Serin's arms, there was a loud *poof*, and he was the size of an ordinary adult cat. He leapt down and rubbed up against her legs affectionately.

'Good, good, it seems he's taken a liking to you,' Durof said with a nod. 'He's prone to biting the heels of people he doesn't like. I can rest easy now.'

Serin ran a hand over Issha's back and his upright tail. 'I've never had a pet before,' she said, suddenly worried. 'What does Issha like? Is there anything I should know?'

'Let me think,' Durof said, stroking his sharp chin. 'As long as you feed him on time, he should stay out of trouble. But . . .'

Serin waited for Durof to break his own dramatic silence.

'Ah, yes. Issha has been hurt by humans before. When I ran across him in the human world, he was starving. Dying by the roadside. Such a pitiful state. I brought him across to the Rainfall Market as a spirit creature.' Then he added quietly, 'But will he be able to reincarnate, I wonder?'

'What do you mean, reincarnate?' Serin asked, having picked up his musings.

Durof sighed. 'Nothing that should concern you,' he said, but added, 'Animals who join us as spirit creatures get a chance to be reborn into the human world. All these little statues here are, in a sense, waiting to be reincarnated.' He gestured to the statues. 'Issha has been here the longest, still waiting to return to the human world. But he can't be reborn until he's received enough love from a human, which he unfortunately seems to have a hard time absorbing because he was so cruelly abandoned in his past life.'

Serin looked around for Issha, wondering if he was listening, but the cat was rubbing his face against a sofa in the distance, and then busily grooming himself.

'But this is no time for such tragic stories,' Durof said. 'Again, this is no cause for concern on your part, Miss Serin. The important thing for you is that you find the Dokkaebi Orb you seek and return to the human world before the rainy season ends . . . Ah, I nearly forgot!' he exclaimed, pulling out a golden antique key from his jacket. 'This key will grant you, holder of the Golden Ticket, access to our finest suite. The bed is so large that Toriya could lie comfortably with arms spread wide, and we offer all the amenities you might find at the finest human hotels. If you require concierge services, the phone in your suite will connect you to me at any time.'

Taking another sip of his still-steaming coffee, Durof stroked his moustache – which came uncurled, then curled right back up.

'Thank you,' Serin said with a bow. As if on cue, Issha came padding over.

'I wish you a pleasant stay, Miss Serin.'

Durof saw Serin and Issha to the door. He stood in the doorway and watched for some time, even after Serin and Issha had disappeared.

Episode 9

The Hair Salon

When Serin woke up the next morning, she wanted to bury herself in the squashy mattress forever. But something prodded at her: Issha the cat. He was kneading his paws against Serin's belly. She picked him up, placed him on the red carpeted floor, and gave the biggest yawn of her life.

A luxurious pair of slippers waited next to the bed, decorated with the logo of a famous brand. The Dokkaebi must have prepared them to suit human tastes, but they looked so fancy that Serin felt uncomfortable. She decided to go to the bathroom barefoot.

'This place is so much better than home.'

Serin hadn't lived in a house with a proper shower in years. The water from the showerhead came raining down, soaking her hair, and she finally felt awake. Although the suite was heavenly, Serin hadn't got much sleep last night, because she was too excited about finding the Dokkaebi Orb of her dreams.

As she had tossed in bed, Serin had wondered what kind of life might make her happy. Then she'd remembered someone: the university student she'd seen on the train to Rainbow Town. Specifically, the school whose name was printed on his books.

Her eyes flew open at the possibility. The reading lamp filled her room with a gentle orange light, and the flower petals strewn across her bed still smelled lovely. Serin got up and poured herself a glass of water from the silver pitcher on her nightstand and decided on a course of action.

I'll go to university and start a new life, she thought, and wondered why she hadn't thought of this earlier. Was it because she'd given up on university so long ago and decided to focus on taekwondo instead? When her classmates got together in their little cliques during break and chattered about which university they wanted to go to, Serin had pretended not to hear, or had left the room entirely.

But now she could dream about campus life. The life she'd only seen in movies and shows.

If only tomorrow would come sooner . . .

Serin saw herself strolling through a university campus. No uniforms, no full-day classes. She could choose her own courses, and spend her free time at extracurricular clubs and make friends she could relate to. She could take on part-time work to save up for things she wanted, or even for an exchange trip overseas.

She swelled, as if that life was already a reality. Serin could think of no better future. Finally, her eyelids grew heavy, and she could rest for the night.

Drying her hair with a towel, Serin looked around for Issha and spotted him stretching near the bed. When he noticed her, he padded over with tail wagging.

Hair still sopping wet, Serin knelt down to meet Issha's gaze. 'I just have to tell you which Dokkaebi Orb I want, is that it?'

Issha wagged his tail harder.

The previous night, Serin realized that Issha was an unusual cat in more ways than one. The abilities that Durof showed off, of course, were one thing. But another curious thing about Issha was that sometimes, he acted just like a puppy. He looked up at her, panting with his tongue hanging out, and Serin wouldn't have been surprised if he'd started barking.

'Just give me one more minute, okay? I need to get ready first,' Serin said. She thought for a moment about what she should do with her bathrobe – she'd never worn one before – and hung it up where she'd found it. As Issha sat quietly, she went to the vanity unit, which was stocked with cosmetics of all kinds, and only picked up the toner and the lotion.

When she looked around, there was an empty bowl in front of Issha. She'd filled it to the brim last night, just in case, but he must have finished all his food.

'You really are a big eater, aren't you?' Serin asked, remembering how Durof said Issha had been starving on the streets. But she was certain she'd poured out enough food for two days, at least.

She picked up the room service menu from the table.

Unlike in the human world, Serin had an abundance of coins to spend. She couldn't use the coins after the rainy season anyway, so she dared to browse through the list of delicacies, finally stopping at the most mouthwatering breakfast platter, which included an omelette, crispy bacon and sausages, hash browns, an apple, a small loaf of bread, and a glass of milk.

Not long after she made the call on the antique phone, someone knocked on the door. When she peered outside, she spotted a waist-high serving cart. From the covered platter on top came a smell so scrumptious that her nostrils flared, trying to take in more. Next to the platter was a bill with her suite number. Serin rolled the cart into her suite.

With a flourish, she threw open the curtains, and was treated to a sweeping view of the world outside. The hotel was surrounded by what looked like a bustling human city, with clusters of colourful buildings. Some were square, while others were triangles or even cones. Yet others were shaped like stars or long diamonds. Even the sizes were all different, as if there was a rule forbidding them from building anything that looked identical to something else. Further in the distance was an endless green field.

Serin satisfied herself with a simple breakfast of bread and milk, and gave the rest of her extravagant meal to Issha.

Just like Durof explained, Issha could eat anything. It was hard to tell how he fit all that food in his tiny body. Scarfing down the contents of the plate like he'd been starved for days, Issha polished off the last crumbs and gave a satisfied purr.

'Say, Issha?' Serin said, wiping the corner of her mouth with a napkin. 'I want to go to a great university. Do you think you can make that happen?'

Issha gave a confident cry. Was it because he knew where to go, or was he simply feeling satisfied after the meal? He bounded to the door, looked back once at Serin as if telling her to follow, and slipped outside.

The sky was a spotless blue, and the sun was almost blinding to behold. It was a lovely morning at the Rainfall Market, and if not for the watch on her wrist, Serin would have thought the rainy season in the world outside was all just a dream.

Not much water had flowed down the little hourglass. Serin still had so much time. She thought back, however, to Durof's warning. How he'd shown the crowd the empty teacup and said, *If you should fail to leave the Rainfall Market before the end of the rainy season, those of you still here on our premises will vanish for all time.*

Reminding herself to never lose her watch, Serin jogged after Issha.

'What a pretty building!'

Issha had led her to a three-storey brick building. It was not large by any means, but the walls were so overgrown with ivy that it looked magnificent. The red of the bricks made the leaves seem even more alive. Serin looked the building up and down, then went to the front door.

A bell rang from overhead as Serin pushed inside. As if on cue, someone chirped, 'Welcome!'

Serin looked up and spotted a figure practically rolling down the stairs. Whoever this Dokkaebi was, she was either extremely impatient or loved greeting customers. *Probably both,* Serin thought.

The beaming Dokkaebi woman was in her early twenties. She wore an apron stained everywhere with dyes, which almost made her look like a painter. And it was hard not to stare at her bright blue hair.

'Hi there,' Serin said. 'I'm here for a Dokkaebi Orb.'

'Oh my! Is it rainy season already?' the woman asked giddily. She gently took Serin by the wrist and led her up the stairs. On the way up to the first floor, the woman asked Serin her name and age, and then introduced herself as Emma, senior stylist at the Hair Salon.

Where the ground floor contained only several cushioned chairs, the first floor was bustling with customers, all with hair caps on their heads and magazines in their hands.

'Please, take a seat!' Emma offered, guiding Serin to an empty chair. Then she began to hum and added affectionately, 'It's been much too long since I've worked on human hair.'

'Er, I'm just here for a Dokkaebi Orb—'

'My, my! Miss Serin, you must remember the rules of the Rainfall Market,' Emma replied, pulling a large, thin sheet over Serin and tying it behind her neck. 'You can't have a Dokkaebi Orb until you've patronized the shop. No need to rush.'

Ironically, Emma was the one rushing to find clips and scissors. The red clip with the rubber clasp at the end, she found easily enough, but her scissors seemed to have gone into hiding. The vicinity of Serin's chair was a mess before Emma finally turned. 'I'm so sorry. Please give me one minute.'

'It's no problem,' Serin replied, although the cloth around her neck was a little too tight for comfort. Meanwhile, Emma lifted up the feet of the Dokkaebi next to Serin for a look, then asked her to get out of her chair. When that turned up nothing, Emma moved on to the next chair along and did the same thing. Serin wondered if Emma wouldn't turn the whole salon upside-down.

'Ahem.'

Serin turned around. Sitting diagonally from her was a Dokkaebi with hair so bushy that he must have never set foot in a hair salon. He looked at Serin with fascination, while next to him was a Dokkaebi who seemed to have no business at the salon, as he was completely bald. But he, like the rest of the patrons, also had a hair cap on his head.

The bushy-haired Dokkaebi said without prompting, 'Hello there, young lady. The name's Burel. The Serenity-Taker. I take away serenity from people's hearts at important moments to make them nervous.'

The bald Dokkaebi, too, said without prompting, 'I take people's decisiveness. My favourite time to strike? When humans ponder over the menu at a restaurant. It's the only joy in my boring life here, watching humans squirm over something so trivial. The name's Vance, by the way. The Decisiveness-Taker.'

Serin didn't know how to respond. But just as she made up her mind to at least tell them her name, Vance the bald Dokkaebi scowled. 'I suppose it's about time for a late breakfast,' he said, his voice rising to a horrifying screech. His eyes glowed red, and his fangs grew longer until he almost looked like a vampire. 'I'll eat you alive!' he roared, the cloth around his neck swishing back like a cape as he lunged.

Serin shrank into her chair, flinching.

Then there was a thud, and something rolled to the floor. Emma had tripped on a hair dryer cord. But the other patrons didn't so much as look in her direction, probably because they were so used to it. Emma, too, dusted herself and came striding over, as if Vance wasn't nearly at Serin's throat, ready to pounce.

'Sorry to keep you waiting!' Emma chirped, holding a slightly dirtier apron. 'Don't let these hooligans bother you, they're only pulling your leg. We Dokkaebi may look a little different from your kind, but we don't eat humans. Our food is almost the same as yours.'

Vance deflated. 'Come on, Emma. I was just having a bit of fun. Now I have to wait a whole year to scare another human,' he complained, making his way back to his chair. Burel gave him a reassuring pat on the back and whispered that the rainy season was only just beginning, that they might run into another oblivious human soon. A smile quickly returned to Vance's lips.

Emma, meanwhile, put on the apron and tied the straps behind her back. At the front was a big, bulky pocket that almost looked like a kangaroo's pouch. Before Serin could ask what the pouch was for, Emma reached in and whipped out what she was looking for: an electric saw.

Serin almost screamed, even more frightened than before.

'Oh! Where is my head at?' Emma laughed sheepishly, and reached back into the pocket. This time, she came up with a small pair of scissors. The blades were half the length of her fingers, perhaps useful for trimming nose hairs. Emma put those back into her pouch, then dug in deep this time, until her entire right arm disappeared.

Finally, she produced a pair of ordinary scissors. Although Serin wanted to ask why Emma had her tools hidden away so deep, she lost her chance because Emma began to jump for joy.

Spraying liberal amounts of water on Serin's hair, Emma brushed out the knots. The tangles and messy spikes quickly hung straight. 'Miss Serin, do you take care of your hair at all?'

'Er, sort of? It's a bit of a bother,' Serin replied, trying not to sound like a slob.

With a hint of a smile on her lips, Emma reached into Serin's hair and snipped. With each snicker-snack, a lock of hair fell to the floor. Serin's hair was short to begin with, but now it barely reached her earlobes. Emma tugged gently at each side to make sure her hair was level, and reached into a drawer on the shelf.

'Emma, did you hear the news?' Burel asked, looking up gravely from his morning paper.

Plunging into the drawer until her head had disappeared, Emma replied, 'What news?'

'Thefts all over the Rainfall Market. They still haven't caught the culprit,' he said. 'Your salon's still all right?'

'Yes, nothing stolen here,' Emma said, finally pulling out a dusty box from the corner. But just as she emerged, she slipped on a lock of hair and fell to the floor. Everyone winced, but Emma rose as if nothing had happened and pulled some hair off her face. 'I don't think this thief would dare, with you and Vance coming by every day.'

'Of course not,' Burel said proudly, not sensing the sarcasm in Emma's tone. He shrugged and flexed his skinny arm, offering Emma a feel. She didn't even look in his direction, instead showing the dusty box to Serin.

'This is a nourishing hair oil made from human compliments,' she explained. 'It's from a long time ago.'

Inside the battered box was an even more battered bottle, inside which sloshed a pale tonic. It looked almost like runny white paint, or whipped cream stirred into water.

Emma checked the best-by date before opening the lid for a sniff. Serin inhaled deeply too, but didn't smell anything.

'Sometimes the compliments are empty flattery, so the hair oil doesn't do anything. It's always important to do a sample test,' Emma explained, spreading a few drops across the back of her hand. She scrutinized her downy hair, and finally smiled. 'Excellent! Genuine human compliments,' she said. Tipping the bottle over, she poured out enough to fill her cupped hand and rubbed it all over her hands before working it into Serin's hair from roots to tips.

'It won't do to leave damaged hair for days on end, so make sure to rub this into your hair every morning and evening. Especially since your hair is so fragile.'

Serin couldn't believe it. Just a few strokes from Emma's hands, and her hair was glossier and softer than it had ever been. And suddenly, she remembered something she'd forgotten.

One day, not long after she started learning taekwondo, she was practising her spinning back kick at the dojo when she heard someone approach. It was the master, the young one with the smile always on his face. For a moment, Serin was worried that her form was off. But she was surprised when he said that she showed real potential.

The master told her that even the boys couldn't rival her skills. Serin had never got a compliment like that before. She looked down to hide the flush on her face. But the master only complimented her more, even giving her a thumbs-up.

As Emma dusted away stray strands of hair, Serin realized that maybe the master had only complimented her to make sure none of his students dropped out of classes. That she had been naïve to believe him. But that wasn't important now. Serin had to focus on getting the Dokkaebi Orb of her dreams

Using a brick-shaped sponge, Emma went on to gently brush away strands of hair from Serin's face and neck. Then she untied the cloth that had been tight around her throat.

Finally able to breathe, and finally sporting the first haircut she ever liked, Serin leapt to her feet. 'How much?' she asked, reaching into her pockets. She hated how they bulged with all the gold coins.

'I'll take two coins for the haircut,' Emma said. Then she put the bottle of hair oil back into its box and wrapped it in a ribbon before holding it out to Serin. 'The hair oil is on the house.'

She also held out a Dokkaebi Orb.

The shiny green Orb was beautiful. Even if it weren't magical at all, it would probably fetch a good price in the human world. With the boxed hair oil and the Orb in either hand, Serin said goodbye to Emma and went down to the ground floor.

Issha was sleeping on a cushioned seat. When he heard Emma and Serin's steps coming down the stairs, however, he gave a massive yawn and padded over happily.

Serin couldn't wait any longer. 'Emma? May I take a rest here before I leave?' she asked, pointing at an empty seat.

'Be my guest,' Emma replied warmly. 'There's plenty of time until I close up shop, no need to rush. And also, the hair oil is very slippery. Be careful not to spill any.' With that, she went back upstairs, tripping yet again on the way.

Serin peered into the Dokkaebi Orb. Tiny particles of light swirled inside, like a miniature galaxy.

Will I really find what I'm looking for in this little Orb? she wondered, and placed it in Issha's mouth as Durof had shown her. She was afraid it might be too big for him, but Issha grew larger so the Orb would fit in his jaws.

Bubbling with excitement, Serin recited the magic spell:
'*Druu epp zulaa.*'

Issha's eyes glowed the same shade of green as the Dokkaebi Orb, and cast light into the room.

A moment later, Serin stepped into a dream.

She stood in the university campus of her dreams.

All around her were green lawns, and standing in the distance were majestic Gothic buildings and ancient trees. The horse-shaped statue rearing in the centre of the fountain looked so real it might break into a gallop any moment, past the flowers dotting the knee-high shrubs that lined the paths.

'Really?'

Serin heard voices behind her and turned. Little groups of young men and women were chattering away without a care in the world, slapping each other on the back and smiling. Serin, though, must have been invisible, because no one even looked in the direction of the solitary teenaged girl.

'Yeah, I saw him lying on the lawn by himself on my way here in the morning.'

A man with short, wax-smoothed hair gave an enthralling retelling of the party for the new students and about how a new professor got lost on campus and ended up cancelling the lecture. The conversation was loud enough to hear, but not quite enough to make out clearly.

'Look at the time! I gotta go in for my shift,' *said one of the students, dusting herself off just as Serin crept in for a closer listen. The others also picked up their things and rose to their feet, bringing up group assignment meetings and dates. Serin stood there longingly as the students departed.*

Ring! Ring!

Beyond the emptying lawn, Serin spotted a young man with horn-rimmed glasses pedalling away on a bicycle. The trees told her it was springtime, but the young man was wearing a thick down jacket.

Something drew her to the man on the bicycle. She followed him, realizing that her feet were gone and she was gliding like a ghost.

The man rode over a small hill and stopped in front of what looked like a dormitory. He practically threw the bike aside and rushed into the building, impatiently stabbing the lift button and glancing at his watch every other second as the lift made its slow descent. He was probably late for an appointment, or had forgotten something important in his room.

Once he was in the lift, the young man took deep breaths. But they didn't seem to help, because his face remained completely rigid.

The second the doors opened, he scrambled into his room, slipping out of his shoes so hard they landed upside-down, and opened up the laptop on his desk.

Serin took a moment to look around the dorm room. It was furnished with only a small bed and a desk, and a makeshift shelf stuffed with textbooks – as well as books on how to write appealing CVs and impress at interviews.

As soon as the laptop booted, the man clicked away like there was no tomorrow.

'Please . . .'

But a moment later, his hand stopped, and his shoulders drooped. The room was so still and quiet Serin almost thought time had stopped.

The man gave a frustrated sigh, his eyes locked on the screen.

On the screen was an email:

We regret to inform you that you did not pass the final interviews. Thank you for your application.

The email went on to describe how sorry the employer was for having to turn down a candidate of such talent, that it was a difficult decision, and that they hoped he would apply again at the next opportunity. But the man's eyes were locked on the first lines of the email.

Loudly, his phone vibrated. The man picked it up in a daze, and found a group chat abuzz with good news from and congratulations for everyone but himself.

He couldn't bear to read any more. The man tossed his phone on to his desk and buried himself in bed.

The phone went on ringing, but the man curled up in his blankets and refused to rise.

When Serin came to, she had no idea how much time had passed. Some more of the water in her watch had dripped down, but not enough to worry her. She tried touching her own face to see if it was still there. Then she looked down, and breathed a sigh of relief to see her legs were back. Issha leapt on to her lap worriedly.

'I'm okay, Issha,' she said, running her hand over his head. Issha gently dropped the Dokkaebi Orb into her hands. The images raced through her mind.

The life in the Dokkaebi Orb did show her the university life she'd dreamed of. But she didn't want to end up like the man who had failed his interview.

Now she knew why Durof said she was lucky to have got the Golden Ticket. If she had taken this Dokkaebi Orb without the chance to look inside, she would have eventually regretted choosing it. She exhaled in relief.

Going to a good university didn't mean anything if she couldn't find a good job afterwards.

'I should think bigger,' she said to herself. 'The whole point of going to a good school is to get a well-paying job.' Nodding, she called to Issha. 'Hey, could I have a different Orb? Let me tell you what I want.'

Issha's narrowed eyes opened wide as he rose, ears pricked up and ready to listen. Serin made sure to enunciate clearly so he could hear:

'I want to join a great company after I finish school. The kind of company everyone is jealous of.'

She must have enunciated well, because Issha immediately

leapt down to the floor. Serin opened the glass door to let him out before he could crash into it, ringing the bell in the process.

'Leaving so soon?' asked Emma, stumbling down the steps again. She waved goodbye with both arms.

'Yes. Thank you so much!' Serin replied, bowing back. Then she rushed after Issha, who was already bounding into the distance.

A second before the door closed, Serin heard another thud from inside the building.

Episode 10
The Bookshop

Issha came to a sudden halt in the middle of the street. Serin almost lost her balance as she swerved to avoid trampling him, and gold coins went flying out of her pocket.

'Issha! What was that for?' she complained, eyes scouring the ground. She spotted a couple of coins rolling under Issha's rump. 'Get up, Issha, I need those coins,' she insisted.

But Issha refused to budge, as though he had been glued to the ground. He appeared hypnotized by something in the distance. Serin followed his gaze.

Ahead stood a rickety old cart that had been converted into a street stand. The tyres were flat, and the cart was so rusted Serin could barely tell what colour the paint might have once been. It looked like a piece of junk – except for the piles of street food stacked inside, which themselves didn't look particularly hygienic.

Issha's eyes were locked on a fried prawn as big as Serin's forearm.

'What's this, now?'

Serin jumped. A Dokkaebi with sideburns that went all the way down his jaws peered out between a pile of corn dogs.

As Serin gaped in surprise, the Dokkaebi raised a finger and pointed a filthy nail overhead.

Does he want me to look at the canvas?

The canvas covering the stand was covered in so many

holes that it barely kept the sun out. And it would help even less in the rain.

'Hey, eyes over here!' the Dokkaebi snapped, and Serin jumped again. Upon closer examination, she realized that he was pointing at a menu made of haphazardly torn cardboard, suspended from a clothes hanger.

He glared threateningly, as if he would turn Serin and Issha into corn dogs, too, if she didn't order soon. Serin flinched and jammed her hands into her pockets for some coins. Then she pointed at the fried prawn for Issha, and the least fly-ridden sausage in the pile. 'I-I'll take those, please.'

The Dokkaebi snatched the coins from her hand and handed over the prawn and the sausage without even putting on gloves. Serin tried very hard not to let her hands touch his as she took her purchase, spotting what looked suspiciously like fly wings dotting her sausage. Fortunately, she managed to force a smile.

The Dokkaebi glared. Serin quickly thanked him and rushed away.

'You're a real glutton, aren't you Issha?' Serin said. 'After all that food you had at breakfast!'

Once the fried prawn was in his jaws, Issha followed obediently after her. *So the Dokkaebi Orb wasn't here after all*, Serin thought. She brought the sausage up to her mouth, and as soon as the street stand owner had disappeared behind the corn dogs again, gave it to Issha. The prawn had already been reduced to a bit of tail. Issha grew to the size of a retriever and swallowed the sausage in one go.

Shaking Issha's spit off her hand, Serin waited for him to lead her onwards. It did not take long. With his longer legs, Issha sprinted off into the distance.

They stopped at a building that looked nearly as old as the street stand. The windows were shattered, and the walls were so cracked Serin had to wonder if anyone lived there at all. In fact, the building was leaning.

But Issha tugged on Serin's sleeve. There was nothing else she could do.

The rusty hinges screamed as Serin pushed open the door. The building was just as run-down as it had appeared on the outside. The paint was peeling and hardly a floor tile was still intact.

Even the run-down house that had led into the Rainfall Market looked liveable in comparison.

At the end of the corridor, however, Serin spotted a light. She followed the glow down the darkened hall.

'Is anyone home?' she asked, peering in through the open door.

The room was full of books. Shelves beyond counting stuffed with one tome after another, with even more volumes strewn across the floor – all covered with so much dust that the titles were unreadable. Cobwebs hung from the ceiling. It looked like a mix of a library and a neglected warehouse.

What is this mess? Serin wondered. Her eyes soon landed on the source of the light – a bright lamp on a table in the corner. Sitting at the table was a Dokkaebi with his face behind a pile of books stacked higher than the tabletop. The Dokkaebi wore a headset and seemed to be humming along to a tune.

On tiptoes, Serin crept through the piles of books and made her way over. Issha, too, crept in her footsteps, shrinking down to a small kitten.

'Excuse me,' Serin said, reaching the table.

But the Dokkaebi did not look up, instead singing even louder than before, so off-key that the singing sounded more like shouting. Serin tried to guess what kind of song it might have originally been.

Just then, the Dokkaebi looked up.

Apparently, the Dokkaebi hadn't looked up because he'd noticed her, because the second their eyes met, he gasped and fell backwards, chair and all. The Dokkaebi then scrambled under the table and squealed, peering over the top, 'Who are you?'

Hoping she hadn't done anything to scare him, Serin replied gently, 'I'm here to buy a Dokkaebi Orb.'

The Dokkaebi looked further up from under the table. Only now did Serin see that he was young, probably the age of a primary school pupil. The horn on top of his head was barely a bump, and there was no hint of a beard on his freckled face.

Only after scrutinizing Serin from the safety of the table did the Dokkaebi finally rise to his feet. 'You're here to buy lunch for me?' he asked.

'I'm sorry?' Serin replied, utterly lost.

Pensively, the little Dokkaebi crossed his arms. 'Well, I like almost everything. Oh, except beans. And aubergines, and mushrooms too. I don't like how squishy they feel in your mouth. And no carrots, either, they're too hard. And I hope you're not one of those barbarians who eat pigs or cows.'

Serin wondered exactly what this Dokkaebi lived on, but realized that he would go on forever if she didn't clear up the misconception. 'I'm not here to buy you food,' she said.

The Dokkaebi replied reassuringly, 'Don't worry, I'll buy us dessert. A Dokkaebi never leaves a debt unpaid.' He reached for the hanger and picked up a brown checked coat, sliding one arm into a sleeve. It was so long that it dragged behind him when he buttoned himself up. That explained why there was almost no dust around the table.

Annoyed and panicked at once, Serin looked around and spotted a small notepad on the tabletop, as well as a feather quill and a bottle of black ink.

Without asking for permission, Serin grabbed the quill, dipped it in ink, and scrawled on the notepad:

I'm here for a Dokkaebi Orb.

The young Dokkaebi had just pressed a bauble-topped hat over his head and was almost at the door when he spotted the note. To Serin's great relief, he seemed to understand and came back to the table. Then he opened up a nearby cabinet and brought out a shiny purple Orb.

'You should have told me earlier,' he said, hanging up his hat and pulling off his coat. 'This is my Dokkaebi Orb. But if you want it, you have to do something for me.'

Serin decided not to remind him that he was the one who'd misunderstood, and wrote down on the notepad:

What do you want me to do?

The Dokkaebi seated himself at his table and pulled off his headphones. Even from across the table, Serin could hear the blast of music. Now she knew why the young Dokkaebi hadn't heard her right.

Clearing his throat, the Dokkaebi said, 'My name is Mata . . . Just Mata,' he added sadly. 'We Dokkaebi are supposed to tell humans what we take from their hearts when we first say hello, but I'm not an Anything-Taker. I've never properly taken anything in my whole life. I'm hopeless,' he sighed, voice trembling. Serin noticed his eyes were watering. 'I told Father how hopeless I feel, but he told me that a Dokkaebi was supposed to make his own decisions once he is a hundred years old. But I'm a hundred and two this year.'

Mata paused and blew his nose into a piece of tissue.

'I've been reading for years, trying to figure out what I might take from humans' hearts,' he explained. 'I want to choose something no one else has thought of yet, something that humans find useful.'

With expectant eyes, he looked up at Serin.

Serin wanted to help somehow, so dipped the quill into the bottle of ink again. But her hand paused over the notepad, because she didn't have any ideas either.

Mata exhaled. 'You know how some people go through the worst hardships but still manage to make their dreams a reality? It's thanks to Father, the Resignation-Taker. He takes away the temptation to give up. He's won Dokkaebi of the Year seven times already. But just look at me.'

Mata curled up in his chair. He looked even smaller now. 'I've tried, really,' he whispered. 'I once tried taking consideration. But those humans only ended up smoking at intersections and talking loudly on the train. It never made a big difference. I want to take something great, just like Father. Something that'll get me Dokkaebi of the Year one day.' Clenching his little fists, Mata added, 'You're human, aren't you? You know much more about humans than me. You have to help me get this right.'

Serin couldn't bear to tell the poor Dokkaebi that she had no idea. But if she gave up now, she couldn't get the Dokkaebi Orb of her dreams. She needed time to think.

Let me try looking for books that might help, she wrote, hoping that would buy her time.

Mata jumped for joy. But just as Serin was about to slip between the shelves, he stopped her. 'Er, who is this?' he asked, pointing at Issha. 'Is this your friend?' Mata climbed on to the table and stared curiously at the kitten rubbing against Serin's ankle. 'He's following after you, always trying to stick by you. My books say that someone like that, someone who stays by your side through thick and thin . . . is a friend. Is this cat your friend?'

Serin didn't know how to explain. She hesitated, but quickly reached for the notepad.

Issha and I haven't known each other long yet, but I think we might become friends. Right now, he's helping me find Dokkaebi Orbs.

Mata answered, 'I see! The truth is, I used to have a friend, too. But we're not friends any more.' He looked like he was about to cry.

'What happened? Did you get in a fight?' Serin asked, realizing too late that she should have written down her question.

But somehow, Mata seemed to have heard her. 'No. But Haku got cross with me one day and stomped off somewhere. We've been friends since we were in Dokkaebi school together.' Hanging his head, he added, 'I don't know what got into him. All I did was toss out his rubbish for him.'

Mata pulled out a wad of tissues and brought them to his eyes just in time to catch the cascade of tears. Serin didn't know if she should stay there to console him, or give him some privacy. He was sobbing so loudly that she didn't know if he could even speak properly now.

Finally, she decided that it would be best to let him cry things out while she went to find the book he needed. All the while, his wailing grew louder and louder.

Serin quietly went up to a shelf and pulled out a book.

Instantly, she knew she'd made a big mistake. The book was written in a language she couldn't read.

The thought of giving up only crossed her mind for a moment. Serin had to check the rest of the books, just in case. She pulled out one tome after another, her hands turning black with dust.

'There are so many books here.'

Some of the shelves were so high up that Serin would have to stand on her toes from the top of a ladder to reach. Many of the books only barely hung off the edge, as though Mata had pulled them out halfway and changed his mind.

The one teetering above Serin's head was one such volume. It was much larger and thicker than its neighbours, and probably too heavy to lift without help. And because Serin was rifling through the shelves below, it quickly tipped over and fell.

The corner of the book plunged straight towards the top of Serin's head.

'Ow!'

Luckily, Serin only ended up with a scraped elbow. Issha had grown to the size of a boar, and a second before the book hit her head, had managed to push her away. He licked her face with a massive tongue.

Serin breathed a sigh of relief when she saw the size of the book that had nearly crushed her. 'Thank you,' she said, wrapping her arms around his neck.

'Are you okay?' Mata gasped, rushing over with one foot bare.

'I'm so sorry, I dropped one of your books.'

'What?' Mata asked, turning red. 'You found the book I needed?'

Serin tried to explain. 'No, what I said was—'

But it was too late. Mata checked the cover of the book first, then went back to the page that had opened when the book fell.

'*The Mysteries of Sea Creatures*,' he breathed, eyes easily scanning the words that looked to Serin like misshapen scribbles. 'The giant clam. When an irritating microscopic object is trapped within its folds, the object eventually grows into a pearl. The giant clam grows to reach 200 kilograms in weight and 100 centimetres in length, and . . .' His voice went silent. Then:

'THAT'S IT!' Mata yelled, skipping around the room and bringing more books raining down. Not caring for his one bare foot, Mata cheered, while Serin tried to wave the dust out of her face and coughed.

Mata went on skipping until he slipped on a pile of books, landing face-first in the pages.

He poked his head out, hair a mess and one nostril bleeding. 'I know what I want to steal now!' he said breathlessly. 'When a human suffers, I'm going to take away the resentment from their heart. That way, they'll be able to endure those hard times, just like the clams with their pearls, until the human's made a beautiful pearl of their own too!'

Taking Serin's hands in his, Mata thanked her again and again. Serin could only smile awkwardly, because she didn't feel like she'd helped at all.

'You've helped me, so it's time for me to help you,' Mata added. The book on marine creatures was bigger than he was, but he managed to heft it on to his head. Now Serin noticed that although he was short, Mata's arms and legs were much larger than she'd expected. 'You have to be careful,' he warned belatedly. 'I once got hit by a falling book, and I was unconscious for two days.'

But when he reached his table, Mata stopped.

'That's funny,' he said.

Serin stood on her toes to look over his head. Mata was furiously shuffling through the books on the floor. One hand steadying the book on his head, he scratched his chin with the other.

Desperately curious, Serin pulled out the notepad again.

Is something the matter?

Mata glanced at the memo and replied gravely, 'I know these books look like a mess, but I know exactly where everything is.' He pointed at a spot under his foot – a curiously clean section of floor. 'If I remember right, this was where I put *The Song of the Rainbow Orb.*'

Serin began to write a response, but Mata seemed to have read her mind. 'Rainbow Orbs are a myth among us Dokkaebi.

They can give their holder anything they desire. Supposedly they're somewhere in the Rainfall Market, but almost no one has ever seen one. Maybe the Chief, and the oldest of the elders. The book contains a song and sheet music praising the Orb, but I think it was nonsense, because I tried singing it once and everyone ran off with their fingers in their ears.'

Serin didn't think that was the song's fault, but did not say so out loud. Mata went on to describe the Rainbow Orb.

'Only humans can use Dokkaebi Orbs, but Rainbow Orbs can be used by anyone, even us Dokkaebi. And it's supposed to be really beautiful, you can tell just from the lyrics. Here, let me sing it for you—'.

Before Mata could begin, Serin scrawled on the notepad:
Are you sure it wasn't stolen?

Mata narrowed his eyes. 'I've heard about all the robberies too. But the thing is, most Dokkaebi aren't avid readers. Actually, I've never seen a Dokkaebi buy a book from my store. If a thief really did sneak in here, why would they have stolen a book, of all things? I could think of so many more valuable objects.'

Serin was in agreement. If she were a thief, she would have robbed a jeweller or a bank. Mata's Bookshop had no security to speak of, but why on earth would anyone make off with a dusty book? As she pictured herself creeping through the dark with a balaclava over her face, she spotted something sparkle between Mata's bare foot and a stack of books.

'What's this?' she wondered, picking it up. The object looked sort of like a gold coin, but she quickly realized it was an intricate accessory. Whatever it was, it didn't belong in a bookshop. She held it out to Mata with a note.

'You found this here?' Mata asked, holding the little object in the light. 'It looks expensive. I don't know much about these things, but it looks like the kind of thing women wear to look prettier. Like from a necklace or a brooch.' His eyes fell on the rectangular spot on the floor. 'If it isn't yours, it must have come from someone else who dropped by. Maybe the one who stole my book.'

The coin-sized ornament sparkled in the light, and reminded Serin of someone: Berna, the owner of the Pawn-shop. She had been covered in jewellery, and Serin wouldn't have been surprised if she dropped a piece or two in a place like this.

'I'll hold on to this,' Mata said. 'Maybe someone lost this ornament, or maybe I could use it as evidence to help find the thief.' He blew the dust off the object and stuffed it into his pocket. 'Okay! Now let's get you your Orb.'

Taking Serin's hand, Mata rushed to the table. He was still huffing and puffing when he presented her with the Dokkaebi Orb.

'I'd love to give it to you for free, but rules are rules,' he explained. 'You have to buy a book from my store.'

Mata handed her the massive tome he'd carried on his head. Serin didn't want to turn down his kindness, but the book was simply too big for her to carry. She hesitated.

'Oh, is it too heavy?' Mata asked. When Serin nodded, he smacked himself. 'I'm sorry, I should have been more considerate. You're not like us Dokkaebi.' He smacked himself a few more times, then reached into a drawer under the table. 'Don't worry, I have just the thing: a Dokkaebi Pouch!'

The pouch was made of leather, and the size of Serin's palm.

Mata demonstrated its use: 'Here, just open up the pouch like this, and bring something up to the opening . . .'

The pouch looked barely large enough to fit the corner of the book, but the second the book touched the opening, it was sucked inside. It reminded Serin of a vacuum cleaner.

'That'll be three gold coins,' Mata said. 'I'd have to charge you seven for the pouch, but this one's on the house, for all your help. I hope you like the Orb.'

Mata brought out a second pouch for the Dokkaebi Orb and handed that one to Serin as well. That meant she wouldn't have to rummage through the one pouch to find what she needed. Serin wished she'd done more for Mata.

Finally, Mata put on his hat and his coat, and walked Serin all the way to the exit. He even offered to escort her out of the Rainfall Market, but Serin stopped him, showing her Golden Ticket and using every gesture she could think of to explain that she would not return to the human world until she had the perfect Dokkaebi Orb. Mata seemed a little sad, but he soon cheered her on, saying that she might even discover a Rainbow Orb.

After multiple goodbyes, Mata finally disappeared into the Bookshop. Serin looked around for a place where she might take a look at the Orb. She and Issha departed, turning the corner round the tilted building.

She had no idea that the thief at the Bookshop had something to do with her.

Or that a gigantic, ink-black spider had been hiding in the shadows on the Bookshop ceiling, watching her every move.

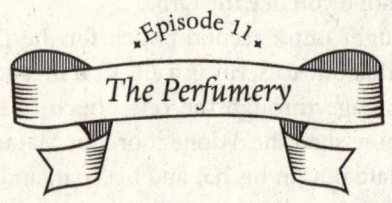

Episode 11
The Perfumery

A red saloon glided smoothly round a corner and stopped in a car park, which was surprisingly crowded considering it was still early in the morning.

A woman in her early thirties stepped confidently out of the car, heels click-clacking with every step. Wearing a beautifully ironed blouse and an entry card around her neck, she was the picture of a driven, working woman.

With what seemed to be a crocodile-leather bag hanging from one shoulder, the woman made her way to a building that connected directly to the car park. Her office was in the tallest building in the busy, bustling city. The whole building was covered in reflective windows and shone like a diamond in the light. When she passed through the large rotating doors, she emerged into an open lobby.

Then she went up to what looked like the ticket gates at an underground station and tapped her entry card at the scanner with a practised hand. The clear gates opened with a mechanical whirr. Serin quickly followed after her.

The lift took them to a floor with an office labelled 'STRATEGIC DEVELOPMENT OFFICE'.

'Good morning,' said the woman.

A weary man looked up with a cup of coffee and a wry grin. 'Morning, chief. Did you get back all right last night?'

'Oh please,' the woman sighed, and added jokingly, 'I get home so late these days the kids barely remember my face.'

Pleasantries exchanged, the man and the woman went to their

seats and quickly started on the day's work. In the meantime, other men and women in similar clothes also arrived and filled all the seats in the large office. Soon the room was filled with the sounds of conversations and footsteps.

'No, this won't work.'

Though the woman had shown up earlier than everyone else to prepare for the upcoming meeting, it must not have gone well, because now she was deleting her documents and starting over from scratch. Throughout the morning, a hard-faced man who must have been her manager called her over multiple times to scold her. The hairstyle she'd set to perfection that morning was already coming loose.

Serin looked around at the other people. They all seemed to be just as busy, talking into office phones or staring grimly at their monitors and files.

'This is hopeless. I should get something to eat.'

At lunchtime, the woman headed to a local restaurant with a younger colleague. The restaurant looked expensive, but the woman must have been a regular, because she did not even glance at the menu before she placed her order.

As they waited for their food, the women complained about their bosses and gossiped about blind dates – then fumed about an ex-colleague who had left the company a year earlier.

'Did you hear about Mingyeong?'

'What happened to her?'

'Remember how she said she was going to start a restaurant when she left? Apparently, it's doing well. Celebrities coming by for meals and everything.' The woman in the Dokkaebi Orb reached for one of the last pieces of sushi with her chopsticks. 'Maybe I should just quit this stupid job and start my own restaurant.'

'But you can't even cook.'

'Who cares? I'm not the one doing the cooking. The important thing is finding the right location, and hiring some cute servers to wait on the tables. Then I can kick back, relax, and enjoy my new life

as a restaurateur.' The woman sighed blissfully. Then she grimaced. '*Should have set some savings aside. Why did I ever touch the stock market? . . . Don't you have some savings?*'

The colleague choked on her rice. '*I-I'm almost broke once I pay off all my loans,*' she replied, panicking.

'*Sucks for us. I hear she makes more in a month than our annual incomes put together. How much longer do I have to slave away here?*' the woman wondered, taking out her compact to fix her makeup. '*Ugh, my skin is destroyed. It's always work dinners and overtime at the office. What good is making all this money if I have to spend it all on hospital bills for all the damage I get from working?*'

As the meal drew to a close, the women each took a toothpick.

'*I'm probably putting in overtime tonight.*'

'*Me too.*'

They sighed loudly, paid for their own meals, and left the restaurant.

The sky was still a clear, spotless blue. The sun, too, remained brilliant and bright, but it wasn't a particularly hot day. An occasional breeze stroked the grass and the branches of the trees, rustling the palm-sized leaves into a relaxing song. Serin knew that if she closed her eyes, she would fall right asleep.

'Meooooow.'

Issha, having just projected a Dokkaebi Orb from the shaded bench under the trees, curled up like a loaf for a nap. Serin, too, was reclining lazily as she stared into the purple Orb.

But she was not particularly excited.

A breeze mussed her hair. But she didn't reach up to tidy it. Eventually, however, she looked up determinedly and found Issha staring into her eyes.

'Issha, I need another Dokkaebi Orb,' she finally said glumly. The purple Orb didn't look as shiny as it had before. 'I don't think I could ever work this hard. I would end up quitting in days.'

Serin plucked a fallen leaf from her hair. Then an idea came to her.

'That's it!' she screamed. Issha flinched and dropped the leaf Serin had tossed aside. 'I want to run my own business.'

She pictured herself next to a window, sunlight filtering through the glass, as she elegantly brewed a cup of coffee. A hint of a smile rose to her face.

'My own business, Issha. That's what I want you to look for.'

Issha jumped gently on to the grass, pressing his nose to the ground. His tail perked up high like an antenna as he sniffed. Soon, he seemed to have a heading. He gave a loud cry and took off. Serin put the purple Orb into the leather pouch and ran after him.

'How far are we going, Issha?'

After enticing him with three chocolate-slathered doughnuts, Serin found herself at the strangest building she'd seen yet. Built right in front of a forest, the building had chimneys coming out from either side, with windows that did not line up with anything, even one another, one on the edge of the roof and another on the corner of the building.

The roof of the building went all the way to the ground, as though someone had set about making a large playground slide but changed their mind and decided to build a house instead. The walls were splattered with all colours of paint, like someone had taken paint-filled balloons to the exterior.

Whoever had built this house, they either had an unusual idea of beauty, or none at all.

'I *think* this is the door,' Serin said. The door was easy enough to spot, but it was lined from top to bottom with locks of all sorts, at least two dozen she could see. Even if she had the keys to them all, it would be no easy task to get inside.

Serin hung back briefly, taking in the building, before finally going up to the metal door.

BOOM!

A second before she could knock, she heard a muffled explosion. Serin screamed and backed away. Issha's fur stood on end. Tendrils of smoke rose from the door and the windows.

And as Serin looked on, mouth agape, the door rattled. Someone was undoing the locks.

'Koff, koff.'

Then the door swung wide open, and a plume of smoke escaped the building. So did a wheezing, soot-covered Dokkaebi. She looked to be about Serin's age, with frizzy hair and goggles just as sooty as her face.

The Dokkaebi finally discovered Serin, frozen mid-flinch outside the door.

'Who're you?' she asked sharply, as though Serin had been the cause of the explosion.

Serin tried to put on her friendliest smile. 'I'm here to buy a Dokkaebi Orb from you.'

'An Orb, is it?' the Dokkaebi interrogated, eyes narrowed into a glare.

Serin shrank, nodding.

'And where's your proof?'

'What?'

'Where's your proof that you're not here to steal from me? That you really are just here to buy my Dokkaebi Orb?'

The Dokkaebi leaned into Serin's face, scrutinizing every inch, then scanned her surroundings. But there was no one else around – except for a cat that had obviously just feasted on chocolate doughnuts.

'I don't have time for customers right now,' said the Dokkaebi. 'I have to stay up all night and then some to replace the stolen concoctions, and I can't risk letting in someone as suspicious as you.'

The Dokkaebi turned on her heels and marched through the door, reaching over to close it behind her.

'Wait!' Serin cried. She took out her Golden Ticket and an Orb from the Dokkaebi Pouch. 'Will this prove it? I'm only here to buy a Dokkaebi Orb, really!'

The Dokkaebi pushed her goggles up to her forehead and squinted at the Orb and the Ticket. She was the picture of gravity, but the fair skin under the spot her goggles had covered made her look comical. She held up the Dokkaebi Orb against the sunlight and squinted harder.

'All right, come with me,' she finally said, tossing the Orb back to Serin. Serin fumbled and nearly dropped the Orb, but managed to slip after the Dokkaebi before the door closed shut.

If it hadn't been clear before, the building had indeed suffered an explosion. Shards of what had once been glass bottles and flasks lined the shelves, and an acrid stench hung in the air.

When the Dokkaebi spotted Serin lingering in the foyer, braced for another explosion, she barked, 'What're you dilly-dallying over there for? You want a Dokkaebi Orb, then come in, buy something you like, then take the Orb and leave!'

The Dokkaebi gestured at a half-destroyed showcase, not even bothering with pleasantries for her customer. Serin tried not to let her annoyance show as she slowly scanned the bottled products. Some were as small as manicure bottles, while others were the size of shampoo bottles. And all of them looked expensive. The products lower on the shelves were relatively intact, and included candles and plastic bottles.

Serin bent down to pick up the nearest candle, which was so big and thick it could probably last all day. The top of the candle was slightly recessed so the wax wouldn't flow out, and a long wick stuck out of the middle.

'Not as stupid as you look, are you?' the Dokkaebi remarked from behind a partition. 'That scented candle? I made it with human encouragement.'

Serin turned, but the Dokkaebi refused to meet her eyes. Her gaze was locked on a lab bench laden with beakers and flasks for what seemed to be an experiment. The faint smell of gas wafted from the lit alcohol burner.

Serin didn't reply. Instead, she went to the next shelf over and picked up a long plastic container.

The Dokkaebi said snidely, still bent over her experiment, 'Oh, that's an inspired choice. Fitting, too. I made that stink spray with condescending words I gleaned from humans. Nothing like it for driving away nuisances like you.'

Serin was quite sure the Dokkaebi could make a stink spray of her own without resorting to stealing from humans. She moved on again, and each time she picked up a product, the Dokkaebi described it without even turning.

Pouting, Serin put back everything but the scented candle she'd chosen at the beginning. The rest of the items were beautiful, but the intricate glasswork would probably cost her all the gold coins she had. And of course, she felt like if she held on to the stink spray any longer, she would end up spraying it in the Dokkaebi's face before she could pay for it.

All right, candle it is.

Serin drew near as the Dokkaebi held up a flask in a latex gloved-hand, scrutinizing the graduations. The Dokkaebi was so focused on her work that Serin couldn't bring herself to interrupt. She had to set her impatience aside.

With all the caution of a mother holding a newborn, the

Dokkaebi brought over a black jar that had been resting at the edge of the lab bench. With a pipette, she squeezed several drops of clear liquid into the pot.

The contents of the jar began to boil. Then smoke. The Dokkaebi and Serin both gulped, transfixed.

Then there was a loud hiss and sizzle, and a pillar of flame burst from the jar, searing the face of the Dokkaebi who was bent over it. Serin heard the same explosion as before.

Whatever the experiment was, it did not seem to be a success.

The flames soon died down to reveal the Dokkaebi's face, which was covered in soot so dark she could blend perfectly into the night, but for some reason her hair was untouched. The Dokkaebi hiccupped, and a cloud of smoke escaped her lips.

Then she growled in displeasure.

'ANOTHER FAILURE!' she roared, and stomped off to a nearby door.

A moment after it slammed shut, Serin heard running water, interspersed with the occasional swear word. The Dokkaebi was probably washing her face. Serin had to cover her mouth to stifle the laughter.

The lab bench was strewn with equipment straight out of a science class. The most eye-catching of them all, of course, was the black jar. Something about it called to Serin, as if it were pulsing with magic.

What could it be? Serin wondered.

She peered into the jar.

Inside was pitch-black darkness, as black as the soot on the Dokkaebi's face. But the moment she looked up, all thoughts disappeared from her mind.

There in front of her was a rainbow-hued Orb, nestled in a box of knick-knacks over the bench.

As if possessed, Serin glided over to the box. She took out

an empty bottle of stink spray, a broken lock, and a greasy rag to dig out the Orb.

'This has to be it.'

The Orb was indeed rainbow in hue, its colour shifting with the angle of the light.

The bathroom doorknob rattled. Serin backed away, panicking, and walked right into the corner of the lab bench. Her backside hurt, but she didn't have time – Serin quickly hid the Orb inside the black jar.

When the Dokkaebi stepped out of the bathroom with a towel hanging from her neck, Serin was frozen in a pose like she needed to go to the toilet herself. The Dokkaebi's eyes narrowed.

'What are you up to?'

'I . . . er . . . I was just looking around,' Serin said, trying to put on a calm front, but a drop of cold sweat ran down her brow. The Dokkaebi narrowed her eyes further and slowly approached.

Serin's heart beat louder than the explosion that had rocked the building. The Dokkaebi strode past her and scrutinized the lab bench, her gaze falling on the black jar. Serin tried to subtly block her way, but could not hide the brilliant glow of the Orb.

The Dokkaebi looked down into the jar. Then her jaw dropped, just like Serin's had when she found the Rainbow Orb. 'What is *this* doing in here?'

Serin shut her eyes. Now she would be kicked out of the Rainfall Market, or worse, accused of being a thief and sent to the dungeon.

The Dokkaebi groaned. But no matter how long Serin waited, the accusation never came. So she let herself sneak a look.

In the Dokkaebi's hand was not the Rainbow Orb, but a thread so thin it was nearly invisible. She didn't seem to care at all about the Orb Serin had hidden in the jar at great cost to her backside. In fact, the Dokkaebi had set it aside on the lab bench – and ignored it as it rolled off the side.

'NO!' Serin shrieked. The taekwondo lessons had paid off, because she managed to catch the Rainbow Orb as it fell. Lying on her stomach on the floor like a baseball player who had made the catch of a lifetime, Serin breathed a sigh of relief.

The Dokkaebi, meanwhile, barely seemed to notice. 'This is a Dokkaebi hair,' she said. 'I knew my theories couldn't be wrong. This hair is the reason the experiments failed!' she declared, putting on her goggles – now so sooty they were the hue of sunglasses – and emptying the contents of all the beakers on the bench into the jar. Finally, she brought out the pipette again and added several drops of the clear mystery substance into the mixture. Once more, the solution sizzled and smoked. Serin huddled beside the bench for cover, plugging her ears.

But the explosion never came. When Serin finally worked up the courage to peer over the lab bench, she saw the jar filled with a substance that sparkled like stars.

The Dokkaebi wore a satisfied smile. Then she flinched, as if she hadn't noticed Serin earlier. 'You! Did you put the Orb in here just now?'

There was no denying it. Serin nodded.

'Thank you.'

Serin couldn't believe her ears. The Dokkaebi continued, much happier than she had been before:

'I wouldn't have noticed this if not for the Orb,' she said, holding up the hair. 'The foreign object that interfered with my experiment.' The Orb must have lit the jar bright enough for the Dokkaebi to spot the hair. 'What's your name?'

'I'm Kim Serin,' Serin replied quickly.

'And I'm Nicole. It's nice to meet you,' the Dokkaebi replied. 'I'm a Word-Taker. I make fragrances from words I take from human hearts.' With her free hand, she offered a handshake. 'Thanks for the help. If I hadn't found this hair, this house would have been in smithereens by tomorrow.'

Serin had to agree. Relieved that she'd arrived before the Rainbow Orb was also blown to smithereens, she took the handshake with her empty hand.

'So why're you holding that thing like your life's on the line?' Nicole asked, spotting how Serin cradled the Orb.

Serin put the Rainbow Orb carefully on the bench and replied, 'Sorry, I'm not here to steal it. I've just never seen a Rainbow Orb before. I only wanted to take a look.'

Nicole frowned, and picked her ear with the hand that had just shaken Serin's. 'A Rainbow Orb?'

'Yes,' Serin said, pointing at the Orb on the lab bench. It looked a little different somehow now, but the hues were still there.

Nicole examined the Orb carefully. Then she burst into laughter. 'Oh! That's one heck of a misunderstanding!' she howled. 'I've never seen a Rainbow Orb myself, but this is just my Dokkaebi Orb.'

Nicole pulled the towel from her neck and wiped the Orb clean. Soon, it turned a brilliant yellow.

'Must have stained it with oil from whatever corner I left it in.'

Serin couldn't believe it. She picked up the Orb and scrutinized it from every angle, but now it looked just as ordinary as the others. She could scarcely hide her disappointment.

'I'm sorry, but the Rainbow Orb's practically a legend even for us Dokkaebi,' Nicole explained. 'Why would little old me have something that precious, you know? Maybe someone much, much older might be holding on to one.' She pushed her beakers aside and gently poured her sparkling solution into a glass bottle. 'Thing is, I just got that Orb myself this morning, so it's practically new. It's not a Rainbow Orb, no, but it's supposed to be really good for you humans, right?'

Nicole was right. Serin didn't need a Rainbow Orb, because Issha had led her to the Orb with the café life of her dreams. She picked up the Orb again. 'So can I take this?'

'Sure. But it's getting late, so you should stay the night here. Weather's supposed to be terrible.'

Serin furrowed her brow. When she walked in, the sky had been lovely and fair. She went up to the window.

It was pitch black. A howling blizzard had come on the town, and Serin could barely see outside even when she pressed her forehead against the window. She would need Mata's coat and hat at the very least if she wanted to venture out.

'That's the weather in the Rainfall Market for you,' Nicole said. 'Happens all the time here.' She yawned, pulling off her filthy lab coat. 'Bedroom's right this way. Keep up if you're not gonna leave.'

Switching to a pair of rabbit-shaped slippers (one was missing an eye), Nicole went upstairs. Serin took one more look out the window before following her, Issha in tow.

The room was by no means large, but had more than enough space to accommodate Serin. Nicole went up to the top bunk and emptied it of knick-knacks, tossing them all across the floor. Then she produced from her dresser a blanket embroidered with carrot patterns.

The ladder up to the top bunk creaked loudly when Serin climbed, as though no one had used it in ages. She put aside the stuffed rabbit Nicole hadn't thrown off the side, gently placing it next to her pillow.

Then she finally managed to ask the burning question: 'Could I ask what you were making back there?'

'Sparkle syrup,' Nicole replied matter-of-factly, changing into a carrot-patterned nightdress.

'What's that?'

'The shiny stuff you saw in the jar just now.'

Serin thought back to the glittering solution in the black jar and nodded, because she would probably have called it the same thing if she had been in charge.

'The sparkle syrup isn't just for perfumes. It also goes into those Dokkaebi Orbs you humans want so much. It's part of the colouring. So I always keep a big stock of the stuff, but some thief broke in a few days ago and made off with my entire batch,' Nicole fumed. 'So I was in a rush to make some more, but my formula just wouldn't work right. Who knew there was a Dokkaebi hair in that jar? I bet it's from the thief.' She held up the hair again, still not having tossed it aside. The strand of hair was at least two handspans long, and curled into the shape of a spring. 'Long and curly, so I assume the thief's a woman.'

Nicole went on cursing the thief, and if even one of those curses were to come true, the owner of the stray hair would have a miserable life waiting for them.

Serin had more questions about Rainbow Orbs, but before she could ask a single one, Nicole was already snoring in the bottom bunk.

Episode 12
The Garden

Serin didn't get a wink of sleep.

The first reason was that Nicole's snoring was loud enough to give her explosions a run for their money.

The second reason was that Serin couldn't wait to see what was inside the yellow Dokkaebi Orb.

When the excitement was too much to bear, Serin quietly roused Issha, who also looked haggard from the loud snoring below. He gave a long stretch, yawned, and took the Orb in his mouth. The world turned a bright yellow as the bunk bed and Nicole's Perfumery vanished.

Serin found herself facing a sleek new building. Then more buildings appeared to either side, forming a narrow, twisting alleyway crowded with all sorts of unique and unusual businesses.

A delivery motorcycle honked as it wove perilously between pedestrians. A couple posing for a picture outside one of the establishments backed against the wall to make way, then stepped forward again to strike a dozen new poses. The alleyway was bustling with excited young crowds.

The show window directly in front of Serin was polished to a shine, but Serin didn't see herself in the reflection. She was like a ghost in this world. She did, however, see the chic décor inside.

Again, she found herself pulled into the building. The café wasn't quite the boutique coffee shop she'd imagined, but it was lovely all the same.

Gentle pop music filled the café, and the menu was packed with mouthwatering pictures of cold fruit bingsu and desserts. Hanging in the place of honour was a laminated autograph.

But though the clock pointed to the afternoon, the café was deserted.

Except for a young woman, who seemed to be the owner.

She sat all alone in a chair by the counter, staring blankly out the window.

Suddenly, her phone rang, and the woman picked up without a second thought. It must have been a friend, because she immediately launched into conversation and grumbled about her life.

'It's awful. I hate it.'

At first the café had been a rousing success, bustling with customers every day. But before she knew it, competitors had sprouted across the neighbourhood, leaving her in the dust.

'I should have just gone into the civil service like you,' the woman complained, going on about how she wished she could have a steady income and not have to worry about paying the rent, then warning her friend not to leave her government job. 'Don't even think about it. How many jobs these days have no overtime and good pension plans? It's all about that work–life balance. I wish I could live like you. Expenses these days are going through the roof, I swear . . .'

The woman looked up. A couple stood outside the door, studying the menu.

'Talk to you later,' the woman said, hanging up. But the couple took one glance at the interior and turned right around, heading to the café across the street.

The owner of the café sank back into her seat and sighed loudly. The world went hazy, and then the fog cleared.

Serin found herself in Nicole's top bunk again, staring at the ceiling with a carrot-patterned blanket and a cat on top of her.

Issha put the yellow Orb down next to Serin and licked her

face. When she ran her hand over his head, he purred affectionately.

Once her face had been sufficiently cleaned, Serin put Issha down and descended to the floor.

'Morning already, huh?'

Sunlight streamed through the window. Issha climbed down, too, and rubbed himself against Serin's ankles.

'I'm sorry, Issha. It looks like we'll have to look for another Orb,' she said. Issha raised his rump high, so she gave him a pat. 'This wasn't the one I wanted after all.' Placing her index finger on her lip, she added, 'I just want to not worry about anything, and be comfortable. Maybe . . . maybe a really stable job?'

With a small meow, Issha leapt up to the windowsill and gazed outside, as though scanning for his next destination.

'G'morning,' Nicole said sleepily, peering up from the lower bunk. Her face was still swollen from slumber. 'Sleep well?' she asked, rubbing an especially large crust from her eye.

'Y-yeah,' Serin stammered. She hoped Nicole couldn't notice how red her eyes were.

With a big stretch, Nicole got up and picked up a carrot-shaped toothbrush. 'Better not go that way,' she warned as she brushed her wide front teeth. 'That's a mischief-tree grove.'

As if in agreement, Issha gave a pitiful mewl.

'What's a mischief-tree?' Serin asked, stifling a yawn.

'What do you think? They're mischievous. They're trees. And a huge pain in the backside.'

Nicole went on to say that one day, she'd use them all for firewood and that if they had noses, she'd have given them a good dose of stink spray ages ago. Then she gargled and spat out a mouthful of water. 'But if you really need to go,' she said, wiping toothpaste from a corner of her lip, 'I can help. Just give me a minute.'

Without changing out of her nightdress, Nicole rushed downstairs. Serin heard the clatter of bottles and jars, and before she knew it, Nicole had returned with a basketful of fragrances.

'Okay, try this one first,' Nicole said, holding out the bottle on the top. She gave the pump a gentle squeeze, and a pungent odour filled the room. 'Essence of sweet nothings. It's the stuff humans whisper when they first fall in love; it'll keep you energized for a while.'

The moment the perfume hit her clothes, Serin felt as light as a feather, as if she could walk on clouds. Issha, too, jumped down to the floor and flopped over in delight.

Nicole reached deeper into the basket. 'Let me see . . . essence of mothers' nagging, and fragrance of white lies about meeting up to hang out sometime soon,' she said, and held out the basket. 'That'll come to a hundred gold coins. What a deal, huh?'

Serin rifled through her pockets, which had got considerably lighter. Though she had spent almost nothing for herself, Issha's snacks had cost more than she'd expected. So she pointed at the scented candle at the very bottom of the basket.

'I think that'll be enough for me.'

Nicole scratched her nose. 'Scented candle of encouragement. It's not bad, I guess. That'll be one gold coin.' She looked disappointed, but didn't try to force Serin to buy anything else.

Nicole urged Serin to stay one more night at the Perfumery, but Serin preferred to get some sleep at night – otherwise she might fall asleep during the day and miss the end of the rainy season. The water in her watch had run a great deal, which had scared Serin so much that she could scarcely stand still as Nicole opened up her door, one lock at a time.

As Serin departed, Nicole handed her a small box. A carrot cake burnt black.

'I suppose it's better than nothing,' Serin sighed. She sat on a flat rock on the road and picked away at the charred bits, which left less than half the original cake – still large enough to count for something.

With the carrot cake in her lap, Serin put a finger in the cream filling and tried a taste. The cream melted in her mouth, and suddenly all her fatigue was gone.

'Wow!' she exclaimed, biting into her first piece. It tasted so good that she closed her eyes to savour every mouthful.

Then she looked down, and her lap was empty. Issha was sitting innocently to the side, his gaze elsewhere. Chunks of cream clung to his whiskers.

Serin couldn't bring herself to scold Issha. She got up and dusted herself off. Her stomach growled loudly, but she didn't feel the hunger.

The forest in front of her was moving.

'What is this?' she gasped, the stolen cake completely forgotten.

The trees had walked out of the earth, slapping one another playfully with their branches. Serin couldn't believe her eyes.

The trees that couldn't possibly have been trees crunched and groaned as they walked. They looked almost like guards who protected the forest, but at the same time like animals in a cage.

Mustering her courage, Serin took a step closer.

Issha growled and padded to her side, growing larger and larger until he was the size of a wolf. He somehow seemed to know that he needed to be prepared, and gave Serin an urging look. Like he wanted her to climb on his back.

But Serin felt like riding Issha would hurt him. And she was confident in her running. Tying her shoelaces tight, she gave Issha a scratch on the back and took a deep breath.

'All right! Let's go, Issha!'

Instantly, Issha leapt into the grove.

The trees quickly turned to follow, but Issha was far too agile. He wove this way and that, and the branches hit nothing but thin air and the pawprints Issha left in the ground.

Encouraged, Serin jumped into the woods after him.

But the trees were much faster than they appeared from a distance. Serin quickly regretted her choice, but when she tried to turn back, the trees had closed off her escape.

'Oh no, this wasn't supposed to happen,' she said.

One of the trees reached out and grabbed her by the ankle. The world turned upside-down as Serin rose up and up, off the ground. She screamed at the top of her lungs, but she knew no one could be around to hear. Even Issha, her loyal friend, was nowhere to be seen.

The monstrous tree shook Serin like a rag doll, and tossed her far into the air. Serin heard the wind whooshing in her ears. She was so high up, and moving so fast. She cradled her head in her arms and screamed.

But the impact never came. It was as if she was lying in a soft bed. When Serin finally managed to open her eyes, she realized that Issha had ballooned to a gigantic size and caught her on his back.

'Issha!' she cried in relief, and slid down to the ground. The trees soon departed, apparently pleased to have rid themselves of an intruder.

Once he was sure Serin was safe, Issha returned to kitten size. She immediately picked him up and nuzzled his cheeks until he could barely breathe. But he didn't seem to mind.

'What is this?'

When she let Issha down and looked up, Serin realized she

was standing in front of a towering tree. It was many times as tall as the ones that had attacked her, branches reaching into the distance and forming a vast shade.

And fortunately, this tree did not move. Instead, there was a small door in the trunk. After everything she had been through in the past few days, a door in a tree trunk didn't surprise Serin too much.

Issha took the lead and went to the door. The Dokkaebi Orb was probably in the tree.

Serin knocked, but instead of waiting for a response, she gave the door a slight push. It opened wide without resistance.

This time, Serin was taken by surprise. Inside the tree she saw a field as wide as her school grounds, lush with trees and flowers. The light shining from somewhere was so bright that she had to squint.

'Hey! Stop right there!'

An elderly woman close to the door was waving her walking stick at a mischief-sapling. But she was so slow that her walking stick hit only thin air. The mischief-sapling easily evaded her blows before scrambling in Serin's direction. Serin panicked and stepped aside, picking up Issha in her arms.

The mischief-sapling rushed out the open door. There was a moment of silence, broken only by the whooshing of the wind through the doorway.

Serin knew she had to apologize. 'I am so sorry,' she said to the old woman. 'Were you doing something important?'

Surprisingly, the woman gave a warm, wrinkled smile. 'Not at all. Please don't worry about it.'

If there was any place likely to have a Rainbow Orb, this had to be it, Serin thought, because the woman looked older than any Dokkaebi she had seen yet. Under her shawl, her hair glowed whiter than freshly fallen snow, and her back was bent so low she was almost the shape of an upside-down L.

'Ah, a human girl, I see. Please come this way,' said the woman, pointing to a nearby table. 'You simply must stay for tea.'

Serin tried to decline, but the old woman was already reaching for cups and tea leaves Serin didn't recognize. However, she was so slow that Serin had to step in and do most of the brewing herself.

As two cups of tea steamed between them, the woman said, 'I suppose you must be here for a Dokkaebi Orb.'

'I am,' Serin replied immediately.

The old woman slurped the piping-hot tea. 'It couldn't have been easy getting all this way,' she said. 'My name is Popo. I'm the gardener here.'

'Oh, my name is Serin,' Serin replied with all due courtesy, hands clasped on her lap.

Popo gave the biggest grandmotherly smile Serin had ever seen, her eyes disappearing in the folds of her wrinkles. 'Welcome to the Garden, Serin. This is where I grow flowers and trees from the unrecognized sweat and tears humans shed.'

Some of the plants Popo gestured to were in magnificent bloom, while others had yet to bud. Serin even noticed a few seemingly dead trees.

'They're all waiting for their season,' Popo explained.

Serin gave her a quizzical look. 'What do you mean?'

Taking a sip of tea, Popo replied, 'Every plant has its season, Serin. Some flowers come into bloom in the springtime, while others wait for summer or autumn. And a few don't show themselves until the coldest winter days, when all the other flowers are frozen. My job here is to nurture them one and all, using the sweat and tears people shed as they strive towards their goals. I make sure that each flower blossoms beautifully in its time.'

Although her missing teeth made it hard to understand

sometimes, Serin could sense sincerity in every word. Taking her teacup in both hands, she asked, 'What were you doing when I arrived?'

Popo chuckled quietly. 'Picking mischief-tree fruits, of course. Toriya is normally here to help, but the poor thing was hurt the other day,' she said sadly, glancing into a grove in the distance. Serin could make out Toriya's big head between the trees, wrapped up in bandages. A bubble of snot expanded and contracted from his nostril as he nodded in sleep.

'Is he hurt badly?' Serin asked, concerned.

'No, it's not so bad,' Popo explained. 'He tripped on a rock as he chased down a thief. The poor thing woke up out of nowhere and said something about catching a smoking Dokkaebi, and fell asleep again.'

Serin almost spat out her tea. 'Someone tried to rob you?'

'You could hardly call it robbery,' Popo replied gently, recognizing Serin's shock. 'Whoever it was only stole a few mischief fruits. They're the Chief's favourite, and they're used to add colour to Dokkaebi Orbs. But no one but the Chief likes the flavour, the poor thief must have been utterly starved.'

With another chuckle, Popo drained the rest of her tea. She set her cup aside and once again picked up her walking stick. 'Please make yourself at home,' she said. 'And let me know when you find a flower you like. I should get back to work.'

For someone who needed to get to work, Popo took an exceedingly long time taking her first step. A less patient person might have snapped watching her slowly rise from her seat. But Serin was more worried about Popo trying to do gardening work with a bad leg, and wanted to repay her for being such a gracious host.

'Maybe I could help you pick those fruits,' Serin offered.

For a moment, Popo beamed. But she quickly waved her

hands. 'No, no. I couldn't possibly take so much of your time. It's all right, I can still do these things myself.'

'Please,' insisted Serin, 'it's my fault that your mischief-sapling ran off, and I need to repay you for the tea.'

Finally, Popo relented. 'Would you, now? Oh, I don't know . . . but if you insist,' she said, not sounding particularly reluctant.

'How much do you need me to pick?'

'Not much at all, only about a handful. But the fruits are so tiny you can hardly see them.'

Serin picked up her tepid tea, which had gone mostly untouched, and downed it in one go. 'It's all right. Please wait here, and Issha and I will get them for you,' she promised, marching out of the tree trunk. Issha rose and followed after.

Serin's bravado faded when she walked out the door and saw the mischief-trees again. When they caught sight of her, they ambled closer. She was never more grateful to have Issha by her side.

She looked over at the wolf-sized cat, still a little nervous. 'Can you do this, Issha?'

Issha gave a lionlike roar.

'All right. Will you let me ride on your back?'

Immediately, Issha crouched down to offer Serin his back. She climbed on and grabbed the fur on his neck, which was now nearly as puffy as a mane.

'We're going to outmanoeuvre those idiots and get those fruits for Popo,' Serin said, and before she could say 'go', Issha was off like a rocket.

Like a pack of hyenas, the mischief-trees swarmed – first only three or four, then dozens upon dozens, as if an entire forest had heard the commotion.

Issha charged fearlessly, and Serin finally noticed the fruits hanging under the branches, very close to the trunks. They were only slightly larger than cherries, so small that she couldn't possibly see them from a distance.

'That's it, Issha,' Serin urged as he got her close to one tree in particular. But the second her fingers brushed the fruits, a bundle of branches emerged and wrapped around the fruits.

Serin and Issha had to step back. The other trees, too, were wrapping leaves and branches around their fruits. Issha looked back at Serin, as if waiting for instructions.

But Serin couldn't think of any. All she knew was that she couldn't give up now.

Was it because she was with Issha? Or because she wanted Popo's Dokkaebi Orb so badly? Or was it the perfume Nicole had sprayed on her in the morning? Serin looked around at the fallen branches and whispered into Issha's ear, 'Do you think you can run faster this time?'

Issha roared so loudly that the trees flinched.

'All right,' Serin nodded. 'Change of plan. If we can't pick the fruit ourselves, we'll make the trees drop them. Show me what you're made of.'

Issha gave Serin's face a lick, as if urging her to hold on even tighter, and launched forward like a bolt of lightning.

Serin was reminded of a rollercoaster, which she had ridden only once when she was younger. But this time, there were no seatbelts or safety bars, and she wasn't speeding on rails. She was on the back of a gigantic cat. She could hardly keep her eyes open, and all she could hear was the sound of massive paws pounding against grass and fallen branches.

Issha seemed to have understood her strategy perfectly. He stayed within the forest perimeter, circling the grove of trees until they were all clustered close together. They swung their branches to grab Issha and Serin, but because they were packed so close, they ended up hitting one another instead.

As branches and leaves tangled, Issha sped past tauntingly. He even dove beneath the roots, squashing himself so flat that he was like a puddle of water. Serin impressed herself with how she managed to keep holding on.

I have to focus, she thought, forcing her eyes open a crack to scan her surroundings.

Thankfully, things were turning out as she'd expected. The trees were so distracted trying to catch Issha that they were crashing into each other and tripping over their roots, some of them falling to the ground as other trees tried to clamber over them. But somehow, though covered in soil, the trees seemed to never grow tired.

'That's enough, Issha,' said Serin. 'Let's lure them far away and go back to Popo.'

With a bark, Issha whirled around and leapt out of the forest. The mischief-trees followed angrily.

It wasn't long before Serin was back at the site of the stampede. She climbed off Issha's back and looked around. They were surrounded by piles of fallen branches and leaves – and little fruits the size of cherries, so many that the world around them looked like a sea of polka dots.

Looking back to make sure none of the trees had circled back around, Serin bent down to pick up the best of the fallen fruit. As it turned out, the fruits were protected by hard shells and most of them were intact, shimmering brightly in the sun.

'How pretty!' Serin exclaimed. She could almost see why the thief had made off with the fruits, because they were lovely enough to be jewels. Quickly grabbing a huge handful, Serin called over Issha, who was happily rolling around in the dirt. He shrank into a kitten again and bounded into her arms. Serin wiped dirt off his nose and turned to return to the door in the tree.

'Huh?'

She had scarcely taken a step when she stopped. Out of the corner of her eye, she'd spotted a dark shape. It was indistinct in form, and didn't seem to have eyes, but somehow she felt as though the shape had been watching her from behind a boulder, peering over the edge.

'I could swear I saw something here,' Serin said, putting Issha down. Crouching, she crept towards the boulder, like a hunter chasing her prey. It was so quiet that she could hear herself gulp.

When she reached the boulder, Serin worked up all her courage and whipped around to the back. But all she saw was the boulder's shadow.

Was I seeing things? Serin wondered, scratching her head of messy hair. Issha, too, sniffed curiously around.

'Let's go,' Serin finally said, picking him up. 'Popo must be getting worried.'

I must be tired, Serin thought. It was true that she hadn't got much sleep last night, and she had exhausted herself playing tag with a herd of moving trees. Without a second thought, she turned back to the tree with the door.

As soon as she was out of sight, there was a hiss, and an ink-black plume of smoke rose from the shadow. The smoke grew thicker and thicker until it was as thick as mud, but with no shape in particular. The lump roiled formlessly, growing larger and larger until it was tall enough to look over the boulder.

It stared into the distance, in the direction Serin had disappeared to.

Episode 13
The Restaurant

Serin winced as soon as she opened her eyes, because the sun was in her face. Still exhausted, she sat up and yawned. Then yawned again. Lying next to her was Issha, head buried in a corner of the pillow and so still and quiet that he could pass for a corpse. Only when Serin placed her ear against his body and heard his heartbeat did she finally relax. Issha sensed her movement and opened his eyes too, giving a long stretch.

Sleepily, Serin looked around. She was in a small room furnished only with a bed with white sheets and a small table. But the pleasant scent of wood from the walls made it better than any hotel suite.

Serin rubbed her eyes and thought back to the previous day. She remembered coming back to the house in the tree, handing over the fruits to Popo, and resting her eyes for a moment. She must have fallen fast asleep.

She was grateful to find a fresh change of clothes and a basin of clean water. Once she'd washed every patch of dirt from her face and changed her clothes, she felt like new. Placing a hand on the branch-woven door handle, she pushed.

A familiar face greeted Serin. 'Good . . . morning. Serin,' said Toriya.

'Toriya! It's good to see you!' Serin replied, taking one of his massive hands.

Bandages were wrapped diagonally around Toriya's head, but he did not seem to be seriously hurt. He must also have just woken up, because a line of spit ran down his chin. Then another face poked out, this time from between Toriya's knees.

'Did you sleep well?' Popo asked with a gentle smile.

Serin gave a deep bow. 'Yes, I did. Thank you so much, Popo.'

She stepped forward, leaning on her walking stick. 'Here. Please take this.'

'What is this?'

In Popo's hand was a small flowerpot, from which sprouted what seemed to be a tiny horn. It was a sapling.

'For bringing me all those fruits yesterday,' Popo explained. 'It may not look like much, but this is the most precious plant in the Garden.'

As Serin studied the plant wondrously, Popo went on: 'I brought it from the human world long, long ago. They call it "bamboo". It's quite funny how for the first few years, bamboo grows so slowly you might think it's died. While all the other plants sprout and grow and flower, and even bear fruit, the bamboo remains almost completely underground, humble and unremarkable.'

Indeed, the bamboo looked more like a piece of rotten wood than a live plant.

'But all those years it spends in the ground aren't wasted, Serin. While the other plants grow upwards, the bamboo spreads its roots deep and wide in the soil, until one day, the roots have all grown. Then the bamboo shoots upward faster than anyone could have imagined.'

Popo turned her gaze upward, to the towering trees in the Garden. One of them in particular seemed to pierce the very sky – a tall bamboo tree. 'Isn't it marvellous? I thought it might suit you well. If you're not looking for anything in particular, I think this would be a good purchase, Serin. It'll only be one gold coin.'

Serin looked down at the bamboo, wide-eyed. It was true that she wasn't looking for any plant in particular, so she had no reason to say no.

'Thank you,' she finally managed to say. 'I'll buy this bamboo.'

Serin placed the bamboo in one of her Dokkaebi pouches and took out a gold coin. Toriya took the coin for Popo in a long gourd bottle he'd taken out of his front pocket. The coin fell with a bright metallic clink.

Popo set her walking stick against the wall and reached into her sleeves. 'Now where did I put that Orb?' she wondered, and finally found what she was looking for.

The Dokkaebi Orb was blue. The slightest hint of disappointment rose to Serin's face.

'I suppose you were expecting something else?' Popo asked.

Serin confessed, 'I was sort of hoping you might have a Rainbow Orb.'

Popo stared in wonder. 'You know about Rainbow Orbs?'

'Not much,' Serin explained, 'I only heard about them by chance, but I know it's supposed to be much better than any other Dokkaebi Orb.'

Popo closed her eyes pensively. 'It's been many years since I heard anyone speak of a Rainbow Orb. There were quite a few to be seen, when I was young,' she said. 'Every Dokkaebi wanted one, because it could make their dreams come true.'

Popo spoke slowly and dreamily, but Serin did not rush her.

'But does anything good ever come of greed? One day, there was a terrible conflict over a Rainbow Orb, and the Chief personally intervened. He took the Rainbow Orbs and split them into pieces, which became ordinary Dokkaebi Orbs. Orbs that aren't of any use to us Dokkaebi. Maybe the Chief missed one or two Rainbow Orbs, but who knows? I haven't seen one myself in a long time.'

'Oh,' Serin replied, trying to keep up a cheerful face.

She clearly failed, because Popo gave her an encouraging smile. 'Rainbows are funny things, aren't they? The harder it rains, the more beautifully they shine. Who knows? Maybe it's a gift from God, for those who've endured the storms. Serin, if you still can't find a Rainbow Orb by the time you leave the Rainfall Market, go and see the Chief.'

'The Chief?' Serin repeated, eyes wide.

'If he could split an Orb into pieces, I'm sure he could put them back into one Orb. The Chief is the greatest of us Dokkaebi.'

'But he sounds like someone important,' Serin said hesitantly. 'Would he want to meet someone like me?'

'You're not just anyone,' said Popo, glancing at the Golden Ticket sticking out of Serin's pocket. 'We Dokkaebi are only allowed to have one Orb each, but you've been given permission to collect as many as you like.'

Brightening, Serin asked, 'Then where can I see the Chief?'

Popo looked over at the closed door, her eyes opening.

'At the highest point in the Rainfall Market. The Penthouse.'

Serin waved goodbye to Popo and Toriya under the big tree as she left the forest. The woods were quiet now, the grove of mischief-trees nowhere to be seen. It almost felt empty without them. Only the occasional fallen leaves made any noise at all.

But soon, Serin crossed a stream and spotted buildings again. She was once more back in the city.

She quickly found a place to sit on the ground and called Issha over, taking out the blue Dokkaebi Orb. It was not a Rainbow Orb, but Serin was not too disappointed. After all, the Orb Issha had found would hopefully have the comfortable, stable life she'd told him to find.

And if she didn't like this one, maybe she could go on

looking for more Dokkaebi Orbs until she found a Rainbow Orb somewhere in the market. Serin smiled, thinking of her new life to come. She felt better already.

Issha was prepared, mouth open and ready to go. It always surprised Serin how at times like this, only his head grew larger.

A blue glow enveloped them both.

Serin was in an office of some sort. She saw large framed pictures and a complex organizational chart on the wall, which meant this was some sort of a government office. The room was big and filled with cubicles – some occupied, some empty – and it was quiet save for the occasional sound of typing. The identical desks and partitions almost made it hard to breathe.

At the end of the office was a different desk, much bigger than the others. The man sitting there slowly rose from his seat and went over to the window, stretching. Then he seemed to do what looked like warm-ups and stuck out his backside and swung his hands together.

It all looked rather comical, but the man was the picture of gravity as he repeated the swings.

'Hello? It's me.'

A few minutes later, he pulled out his phone and made plans for a game of golf, the conversation getting longer and longer until he pulled out a pack of cigarettes from his desk and walked out of the office, still chatting.

A petite woman was watching it all.

She sat at a corner desk, apparently hard at work on something, but took her hands off the keyboard as soon as the man was gone. Her monitor displayed a blank document with a blinking cursor. The woman's face was reflected in a small mirror on the desk.

She looked to be in her late twenties, and was dressed and made up as nicely as a newscaster. But she looked just as stiff as the rest of the office, making even her bright red lipstick seem lifeless.

Serin went to her and found that she was chatting on a messenger app on the computer. The conversation read:

What are you doing after work?
Out with the bf. What's up?
Ok, are you busy this weekend?
I'm off to europe for a month, I told you.
I didn't know it was this week. How long are you gone?
1 month
Lucky you. Get me a souvenir and let's hang out when you're back
Sure, take care
You too

Huddling behind the computer monitor, the woman scrolled on her phone, hidden on her lap.
She sighed.
Each time her clear-varnished nails scrolled down the screen, pictures went flying past.
And her sighs turned to gasps of awe.
Every picture featured a different exotic travel destination, and a man with the physique of a model. He sported a healthy tan and wore his sunglasses on top of his head. Next to his photos was a small profile section:
Travel writer.
The man looked so happy, so unlike the office workers trapped in their lifeless grey building.
He was snorkelling in emerald-hued waters, rippling muscles and tan and all, and lay under a palm tree on the beach with a coconut in hand. The picture of him jumping off a plane with a parachute strapped to his back was both terrifying and exhilarating.
'When am I going to go on a vacation like that?'
Longingly, the woman pressed 'like' on every picture. Then she put away her phone, and her face was lifeless once more.

The owner of the large desk returned to the office, still practising his golf swings. The woman quickly looked up at her monitor, but the cursor went on blinking on the blank document.

The world went dark, like a cinema after a film.

Then the world was bright again, and Serin shook her head. She was back in the Rainfall Market. It seemed that the visions she saw in some Orbs lasted longer than others. Serin considered asking Durof why, but didn't want to go to all the trouble.

Issha spat out the now-slimy blue Orb.

'Hey, Issha,' Serin said, picking up the Orb with only her thumb and index finger and dropping it into her pouch. 'I just realized, what I really want is freedom. I want to go anywhere I please, instead of being stuck in one place forever.'

She felt a little guilty about changing her mind so much, but Issha didn't seem to care. His rump waggled excitedly, tail moving so fast it was a blur.

'I'm not annoying you, am I?' Serin asked.

But instead of answering, Issha pressed his nose against the grass and sniffed. Soon, he had a heading and bounded off with his tiny legs.

Serin rushed after him, quickly disappearing into an alley.

With a gulp, Serin looked up. She had never seen a building like this one. It wasn't simply large. The windows, the doors, and even the mat outside the entryway were giant-sized.

It looked almost like the strongest Dokkaebi in the Rainfall Market had forcibly stretched out the entire building, or someone had cast some sort of enlarging spell on it. Or had Serin and Issha got smaller?

Whatever the case, the building looked less like a home and more like an architect's model.

And as if specifically to prove her wrong, the door opened and a Dokkaebi large enough for the door emerged. He was so big that Toriya was a child in comparison.

'Whoa! Holy smokes!' he cried, narrowly missing Serin as he swung the door open.

The Dokkaebi wore an eyepatch and a hat embroidered with a horrible skull. If not for his frilly apron and flowery ladle, Serin would have turned and run instantly. A nametag on the apron identified the Dokkaebi as 'Bordo'.

Bordo knelt to meet Serin's eyes. 'What's this now, a human? What're you doing here?'

Before Serin could respond, another face – identical to Bordo's – popped out of the building. But this one looked kinder, probably because he wasn't dressed like a pirate. 'Bordo, you dimwit, it must be raining in the human world. It's about that time of year.'

Bordo held up his fingers to make a quick count. 'Huh. Time sure flies, eh?'

'Tell the human to come in and have a look.'

With a doubtful look, Bordo leaned in close and warned Serin, 'Better not make trouble here, you hear me?'

'Er . . . right,' Serin replied stiffly, and looked up. She finally noticed the gigantic sign over the door.

In equally gigantic letters, it read:

Bordo and Bormo's Restaurant

The restaurant was packed.

The moment Serin stepped through the door, the heavy smell of food pierced her nostrils. The air was thick with conversations and the sound of cooking, almost like an open-air market. Occasionally someone raised their voice, but they did not seem to be fighting.

Careful not to get trampled by drunk Dokkaebi, Serin made

her way inside and spotted an empty chair nearby. But it was so big that it looked more like a massive scaffold.

'Well, well, well! If it isn't a little human girl!' the Dokkaebi in the next seat snickered, bringing a handful of crisps to his mouth. He was just as large as Bordo, and crumbs from the crisps littered his bushy beard. His blue Hawaiian shirt was so tight against his chest that he might send the buttons flying with one wrong move.

The Dokkaebi held out his arm, which was the size of a log. 'Nice to meet you, the name's Hank. I'm the Wash-Taker, I take away humans' desire to wash on their days off.'

He extended his hand to Serin, who had flinched, then awkwardly realized he wasn't trying to hit her. She accepted his handshake. 'It's nice to meet you. My name is Serin.'

After the handshake, Hank brought his hand down all the way to the floor. Serin climbed on to it, and he lifted her with ease all the way to the empty seat.

'Thank you.'

The moment Serin sat, Bordo emerged again, holding a tankard so big she could bathe in it. He slammed it on to the counter in front of Hank, sending droplets flying everywhere. Serin was soaked.

Without a word of apology, Bordo shot at Hank, 'All right, so what's keeping Bill today?'

Hank knocked back his drink, gulping ravenously, and tossed a handful of peanuts into his mouth for good measure. Then he replied, 'Busy with the Inn, apparently—' and the rest was so garbled with food that Serin couldn't make it out.

'What?' Bordo said sharply, incredulous. 'The place is *never* busy.'

'Normally, no. But it's the rainy season, all the humans need some place to stay,' Hank said, between belches. Serin smelled rotten eggs and sewage, and had to clap a hand over her mouth.

'Says he's worried. Something about some humans going missing.'

Serin hadn't meant to eavesdrop, but Hank's remark instantly erased all thoughts about his stinky breath. She felt a little guilty but told herself that she couldn't not eavesdrop, with how loudly he was talking.

'Probably got their Orbs and headed home,' Bordo replied with disinterest.

'The thing is,' Hank said, 'Bill says they usually stay all season. And weirder still, they left all their things in their rooms.' He reached into the corner of his mouth and picked out a scrap from what could only have been the Stone Age. The ancient spinach narrowly missed Serin on its way to the floor.

'Eh, I'd bet they're at Gromm's. Wouldn't be the first to get stuck here gambling.'

'Anyway, he's staying behind to watch their stuff, just in case.'

'He's a bleeding heart, that Bill,' Bordo groaned. Then he finally spotted Serin, who could barely poke her head above the counter. 'What're you still doing here?' he demanded, waving his flower-print ladle menacingly. 'You've had your look, now leave. I'm busy at the moment.'

'But I'm here for your Dokkaebi Orb.'

'Well, why didn't you say so?' Bordo snapped. He scratched his neck with the ladle. 'Where did I put that thing?' he muttered, then said, 'Anyway, I'm busy. Come back later.'

Then he walked off before Serin could say a thing.

'Sorry about Bordo,' Hank said, utterly drunk. 'You gotta understand, there's gonna be a big party soon, and he's running the eating contest. It's practically the main event.'

Hank hiccupped, holding his tankard upside-down over his mouth. As if on cue, the ground quaked.

'Here they come.'

A crowd of towering Dokkaebi, each of whom could barely fit in the door, pushed into the restaurant. From the looks on their faces, they looked like they were here for a scowling contest.

The Dokkaebi with the biggest scowl of all slammed a fist on the counter.

'BORDO! Where's the grub, my man? Should've had it all ready for us!'

Bordo rushed out of the kitchen, holding a platter laden with food.

'No more of your cheek, Dunkie, just don't spew up your food halfway like last time.'

Dunkie's scowl somehow grew more ferocious. 'You mark my words, this time will be different . . . Where's Bill?'

This time, it was Bordo's turn to scowl. 'Busy with some business or other.'

Dunkie gave a roar of laughter. 'Bill's out? Looks like Dunkie's Restaurant has this year's eating contest in the bag!'

The crowd of Dokkaebi stirred, and one of them – a Dokkaebi whose belly threatened to spill out of his trousers – stepped forward. 'Hah! The Roland Company's taking first prize today.' Noting the size of his gut, Serin internally agreed, but then she spotted the two-headed Dokkaebi next to him and quickly changed her mind.

As Serin scrutinized the participants, changing her guess of winner each time, Bordo finished preparing for the competition.

Each seat at the table, except for the one labelled 'Bill', was served a veritable mountain of meat – so much that it would make most people sick before they took two bites. The competitors sat waiting for the signal as though preparing for war.

Even the other patrons, who had been drinking at their seats, picked up their cups and gathered around the table. It wasn't long before the murmurs died down, and all eyes fell on the bell in Bordo's hand.

Bordo took a big breath and—

'Wait!'

A tiny voice broke the silence. All eyes fell on Serin.

'Please let me join too!' she cried.

Everyone fell quiet again. Then one Dokkaebi burst into laughter, then another, until the whole restaurant was howling. One Dokkaebi was nearly crying, and Bordo's head was thrown so far back that he could barely breathe.

Before Bordo could die from laughter, Serin added, 'If I pay a gold coin to join, you'll give me your Dokkaebi Orb, right?'

'*You*? Join the *eating contest*?' Bordo managed to reply.

'Yes,' Serin nodded. 'You have an empty seat.'

Dunkie chuckled. 'Why not, Bordo? Make things challenging for the rest of us!'

The Dokkaebi with the bulging gut fell over laughing, and Serin once more covered her ears as the rest of the patrons laughed their heads off.

As the uproar continued, some Dokkaebi joked that they should humour Serin and let her take Bill's place. Bordo did not bother to settle them down.

'All right, then. One gold coin, and you get to take Bill's place. And not like this concerns you, but it's a hundred gold coins for the winner.'

With Hank's help, Serin took Bill's seat at the table. Now that she was up close, she felt a surge of regret – the plates were stacked with more meat than she had eaten her whole life – but it was too late to pull out of the competition now.

Bordo rang the bell.

Before she knew it, the restaurant was filled with the sound of chewing. Serin quickly dug in. She hadn't eaten anything recently, unless you counted the tea in the Garden, so she didn't need to chew very hard to get her food down. But it wasn't long before she reached her limit. Feeling as though her food was forcing itself back up to her mouth, Serin looked around. The two-headed Dokkaebi next to her was ravenous, devouring his food like no tomorrow.

'That's not fair!' Serin cried without thinking. 'He might as well be two people!'

Bordo took his finger out of his nostril and half-heartedly wiped it on his apron. 'Them's the rules. If you can get through that door at the same time, you count as a team. Tough luck, Missy.'

To everyone's shock, Serin looked Bordo fiercely in the eye. 'Then I do have a teammate!'

'Oh yeah? Where?'

Bordo looked around, finally laying eyes on the bottom of the table. He spotted a small, squirming figure – a kitten so small it could fit snugly in Serin's pocket.

With a seasoning-stained hand, Bordo pointed. 'You mean that puny stray?'

'He's not a stray! His name is Issha,' Serin replied indignantly. 'He's always with me, even when I walked through those doors! So we can compete as a team.'

Bordo's brow wrinkled as he took out an anchovy from the broth and tossed it Issha's way. Issha could barely fit the fish in his mouth, nibbling away with paws around the tail. Bordo snorted so hard that snot came shooting out his nose. Wiping it on his apron, he declared, 'All right then, see if your kitten makes a difference. But you better hurry, time's running out.'

'You mean it?' Serin asked, facing a chunk of steamed rib so large that it was as good as new, in spite of all the bites she'd taken.

'What do you think we are? Humans? Start working on your food, or you'll be here until next year's rainy season.'

The other patrons burst into laughter again. Red-faced, Serin rose from her chair. But instead of giving up, she went up to Hank, and pointed at the cupboard against the wall. 'Hank, could you please put me on top of that cupboard?'

'Up there?' Hank asked incredulously.

'Yes.'

Hank looked up at the cupboard again. It was filled with spices and seasonings. 'The ribs too bland for you?'

'No, there's no time to explain. Quickly!'

Hank asked nothing more, lowering his hand so Serin could step on it. She did, and called over Issha.

'Come here, Issha!'

He swallowed the remains of his anchovy and rushed to Serin, leaping into her arms.

'I didn't want to do this, but we have no other choice,' Serin said, looking Issha in the eye. 'Durof was telling the truth about you, right? He wasn't using some magic trick?'

'Meow.'

'This is the only way I can make you use your powers to the fullest, right?'

'Meow.'

'And it's not going to hurt you, right?'

Each of Serin's worried questions was met by the same meow, even as Hank slowly raised them up to the cupboard.

Safely among the dipping bowls and pepper shakers, Serin looked down. She felt like she was on top of a skyscraper. She took a deep breath.

The patrons were looking up at her now. Bordo was still picking his nose, and Hank nervously stroked his beard. Even the other competitors paused with chunks of meat halfway to their open mouths.

Serin raised Issha over her head. 'Are you ready?'

'Meow!' Issha cried confidently.

Serin closed her eyes and let him go.

A stunned silence fell over the restaurant.

Slowly, Serin let herself open her eyes. Several Dokkaebi had risen from their seats in horror. And below, Issha had thankfully landed with ease, and was growing larger and larger by the second, faster than she had ever seen him grow. Soon he was towering over the Dokkaebi, rising up and up until his head was nearly touching the ceiling.

The silence grew louder.

Someone dropped a tankard of beer, but no one seemed to notice or care.

Bordo's finger slid so deep into his nostril that it bled, and Hank was now stroking the hair of the Dokkaebi sitting in front of him. Beer spewed from more than a few lips, and the competitors were so slack-jawed their food was rolling out of their mouths.

Serin alone was smiling, triumphant. She declared loudly, 'One big bite, Issha! Let's go!'

Episode 14

The Curiosity Shop

Serin had to pay quite a bit in damages because Issha had swallowed up the table and plates in addition to all the meat for the competition, but she still had more than enough to spare. She also had her winnings.

Together, Serin and Issha made it on to the wall of fame, leaving a handprint and pawprint respectively.

Bordo tapped her on the shoulder. 'Not too shabby, Missy. Thanks to you, the restaurant gets to keep the champion's crown.'

Serin felt proud, but also a little disgusted because she knew where that particular finger spent most of its time.

'And good news! I remembered where I put that Dokkaebi Orb.'

Bordo took off his hat. Nestled there on top of his head was a red Orb.

A Dokkaebi with the nametag 'Bormo' emerged from the kitchen. 'I must've gotten all the brains in this family,' he sighed. Serin realized he was probably in the kitchen the whole time.

'It's all your fault,' Bordo accused, pointing at his twin. 'My memory would be just fine if you didn't steal so many memories from humans and pack them into the food. Especially after the Chief said not to take more than we need.'

Bormo backed away from Bordo's finger. 'Look, Bordo. The only memories I take are the bad ones humans *want* to forget.' Then he paused for a moment and added, 'Although I admit that sometimes I get too enthusiastic and they forget something important. Only sometimes,' he said, pinching his thumb and index finger together. Then he added, 'But mostly it's Bordo's fault.'

'Hey!'

'You're the one who takes old memories from people so they don't remember what it was like to be young,' said Bormo. 'I still remember the day I was born, and learning to walk.'

Tut-tutting, Bordo retorted, 'They'd never get married and have kids of their own if I let them keep those memories. They'd know how hard it is to raise children, which means we'd run out of humans to steal memories from.'

'I can't believe you thought that far,' said Bormo.

Bordo plucked a stray hair from his nostril. 'Course I have. Humans should be thanking me, because I'm the only reason they're still around.'

The twins high-fived, in agreement for the first time. But Bormo grimaced and immediately headed back into the kitchen to wash his hands.

Before Bormo came back and the Dokkaebi started another argument, Serin rose from her seat. 'Thank you for the Orb.'

'Hold it, don't forget your food,' said Bordo, also scrambling out of his chair. Then he held out a plastic bag Bormo had left behind. Inside was a loaf of garlic bread and a container of olive oil. 'Made this with humans' memories of being babies,' he said, reaching in to show the loaf, but Serin snatched the bag away in horror before he could touch anything.

'Thank you both. I'm really grateful.'

As Bordo went back to picking his nose and Bormo wiped

his hand on a face cloth, Serin strode out the towering restaurant doors.

A man sat in an exotic hotel room, his face buried in the desk.

There must have been a wild party the night before, because the expensive-looking wooden desk was a mess of empty champagne and wine bottles, as well as entire plates of snacks and meals. It was a sight Issha would have jumped at.

Then there was a flash of light, brighter than anything the hotel lights could have produced. Fireworks were exploding outside, scattering colourful sparks everywhere and bringing more of the room into view.

The room was large and had two beds. One of them was occupied by a suitcase covered in barcode stickers. Clothes hung haphazardly from the edges, and a pair of sunglasses had been left upside-down on the top.

The desk was a mess of Polaroid pictures that hinted at the man's occupation. He was at the centre of every photo, smiling among people of all ages, ethnicities and genders in every backdrop and outfit imaginable.

Then, the man muttered:
'Please . . . don't leave me . . .'
Serin scrutinized the man. Sticking out under his arm was an open notebook. The handwriting was a mess, probably because the man was drunk when he wrote the words. Thankfully, she could still make it out. The notebook must have been a journal.

I heard she's getting married.
I was sure I'd moved on. So why does it hurt so much?
I thought I'd forget her if I kept busy and ran away.

I can hardly believe how long it's been.
Is this really the life I've always wanted?
Was it really right to break up with her for my dreams?

Did I really succeed?
What is success, anyway?
Why does my life feel like a complete failure?

The page ended there, but Serin couldn't resist. She gently pulled the whole notebook from under the man's arm, which revealed a mobile phone. The phone was low on batteries, but the screen still showed the photo the man must have been looking at before he fell asleep.

My friends look so happy in all their pictures.
All I have now is myself. All alone.
How do I even fill this void?

I miss her more than ever today.
Why didn't I appreciate her more? I wish I'd known how much
   I would regret letting her go.

If only I could go back in time. I wish I could be with her again.
I would give anything for that chance.

The rest of the page was too soaked in tears to make out. In his sleep, the man called out someone's name, again and again. The page grew more and more soaked.

Slowly, Serin set down the red Dokkaebi Orb.
   Issha padded over and licked her face.
   'Oh, Issha,' she whispered. The life in the red Dokkaebi Orb left a heavy lump in her chest, as though she were the one who regretted breaking up with a loved one. The loneliness in the pages seemed to echo through her heart.
   As Issha rubbed up against her chest, Serin stroked his back and said, 'I'm really sorry, I really am. But I want a different Dokkaebi Orb.' Running her hand down his soft fur made her

feel a little better, but the aching loneliness from the previous Orb still stung. 'I want to marry the person I love.' Blushing, she thought of the boy from the taekwondo class and added shyly, 'Someone tall and handsome, if that's okay.'

Issha rubbed against her several times before he leapt from her arms and went on his way. Serin followed him once more.

The massive buildings soon gave way to normal-sized ones, which looked like toys in comparison. But Serin soon realized that the smaller buildings were, in fact, toy houses.

What she'd taken for bricks turned out to be toy blocks, the same kind she used to play with when she was little, and the roofs were made of chocolate tiles.

Issha entered one of the buildings, making sure to take a big bite out of a cookie door before Serin could try to stop him. Hoping repairs to the door wouldn't cost too much, she rushed inside.

The house was packed with toy clowns and balloons, like there had been a party only moments earlier. Either that, or the house was a party store. Serin saw plenty of other toys, too – everything she had wanted when she was a little girl.

One of the toy clowns moved.

As Serin gasped in horror, the toy clown blinked and stepped forward.

'Hello. Is this your first time here?' he asked.

The Dokkaebi, who had been utterly motionless and unblinking until now, wore Groucho glasses and a party horn in his mouth. The party horn unrolled with a loud squeak each time he spoke.

'Welcome, young human!' he cried, setting off a party popper. A clockwork monkey loudly played a pair of cymbals until it lost its balance and fell on its back. It was a shabby welcome indeed.

Dusting confetti from her shoulders, Serin replied, 'It's nice to meet you. I'm here for a Dokkaebi Orb.'

'I see!' the Dokkaebi said. 'It's nice to meet you, my name is Panko, and I am the Curiosity-Taker! Please take your time, my store is full of excitement and curiosity!' he said, gesturing at the shelves. He pointed at one in particular and added, 'Here is my pride and joy, the Dokkaebi Orb—'

Panko paused, his breath caught in his throat. The party horn fell out of his mouth.

'No, I swear I put it right here,' he stammered, bending down to check the floor until the back of his underwear was showing. But he came up empty-handed, looking more panicked than ever. Serin began to suspect that the thief had made their way here, too.

'I oughta ground that boy!' Panko snapped, seeming to realize something.

'Did someone steal from you too?' asked Serin.

Pulling out the few strands of hair still on the sides of his head, Panko replied, 'I am terribly sorry, I should have kept an eye on that silly boy.'

'No, not at all. You know who took the Dokkaebi Orb?'

'You see,' said Panko, 'my grandson was just here to visit. I think he must have taken it, the rascal. He's got a habit of nicking things that don't belong to him. My sincerest apologies, I've raised the boy poorly.'

Panko took off the Groucho glasses for a moment to dab at the corners of his eyes – revealing that the glasses were simply glasses, and the joke nose was actually his nose. A surprised Serin asked, 'Do you know where he is?'

'His father's Scrap Yard, I believe. I've raised the boy poorly—' Panko said, falling to his knees and pressing his forehead to the floor.

Serin tried to pull him back up and replied, 'It's all right. Issha here will help me find it.'

'Ask for help from a customer? I couldn't possibly! I've raised the boy poorly, it's all my fault,' Panko said in a muffled voice.

'Really! It's all right!' she assured him. 'Issha has a sensitive nose, he'll find it in a flash! Right, Issha?'

'Meow!' Issha said confidently.

'Issha wouldn't have come here if the Dokkaebi Orb wasn't here until just now,' Serin added. 'So please, don't worry. And no need to grovel, either.'

Panko looked up at Serin, teary-eyed. 'Th-then . . . you forgive me?'

'Of course I do! There's nothing to forgive at all!'

Panko burst into tears, sobbing until his handkerchief was soaked through. Then he pressed his forehead against the ground again.

'My poor grandson Haku lost his parents when he was a wee boy. I raised him myself while I ran this Curiosity Shop. I simply didn't have the time to devote to taking human curiosity, so some humans still haven't lost their taste for toys even when they're adults. I've done poorly.'

Serin gently pulled Panko back up. She wasn't quite sure if she had any right to be forgiving Panko, but she had to calm him down. 'Please, you've done nothing wrong. And even if you have, I forgive you, all right?'

'Oh, how generous of you!' Once more, Panko burst into tears of gratitude.

As he slowly regained his composure, Serin said, 'Issha and I will go look for the Orb now,' and rushed away. She was afraid that if she stayed any longer, Panko was liable to bruise his forehead against the floor.

Putting his ordinary glasses back on, Panko followed Serin

to the door. 'Thank you. You've saved my life. Truly,' he said, bowing so low that his nose nearly touched the ground.

Serin bowed back, as low as she could. 'Not at all. Please take care.' Then she went on her way, looking back again just to make sure he hadn't prostrated himself one last time.

Episode 15
The Scrap Yard

Haku was not difficult to find.

Issha led her to a yard heaped with discarded parts. But no one can have been taking care of it, because the fence around it was punched full of holes, the ground was overrun with weeds, and a horrible stink filled the air. Serin looked past the faded sign reading 'SCRAP YARD'. The yard ahead looked like a rubbish dump. It went on to the horizon, with mountains of scrap rising high into the air – some so high that Serin would need hiking shoes and a walking stick to reach the top.

Finding a young Dokkaebi here would be like finding a needle in a haystack. Serin had Issha for help, of course, but the stench was so overpowering that he seemed to have trouble locating the Orb. Issha circled round and round the same spot, near a cave in the heap that looked like a rabbit hole.

'Are you sure this is the place, Issha?' Serin asked hesitantly.

'Meow . . .' Issha replied, more uncertain than ever before.

'I suppose there's only one way to find out.'

As Issha waited with his tail limp, Serin strode forward and climbed inside.

The cave was pitch-black.

Serin reached into a Dokkaebi pouch and pulled out the first Orb that she could find. It wasn't quite as strong as a flashlight, but it was enough to help her see.

That, however, didn't help the terror. Or the stench. The

light only made it clearer just how precariously the junk was balanced, and the smell only grew stronger as she walked.

The floor of the cave was flat and the passage didn't get wider or narrower as she went, meaning that someone had dug it on purpose. But the cave was so narrow to begin with that Serin couldn't walk, even if she hunched forward, and had to crawl on her knees instead.

To her great relief, the cave quickly gave way to an opening.

Inside was a small, cavernous room tall enough for her to stand, lit by a faint glow – a glow just like the one from the Dokkaebi Orb in her hand. Knowing what she would find, Serin marched forward.

A small Dokkaebi sat curled up in the little room. He wore no shirt, although Serin didn't know if this was because it was too hot or that he simply didn't like shirts, but he did wear a worn bow tie around his neck. His trousers were so tattered that Serin almost took them for rags.

The Dokkaebi didn't seem to notice Serin enter the room. His eyes were locked on the Dokkaebi Orb, whose faint glow could light up the entire room.

'Ahem,' Serin cleared her throat.

The Dokkaebi finally realized that he wasn't alone. He turned, and jumped with a scream.

The scream scared Serin almost as badly as the Dokkaebi. He went on screaming himself hoarse, but refused to let go of the Dokkaebi Orb. Quickly returning to her senses, Serin tried to soothe the young Dokkaebi. 'Hey there, it's okay. My name is Serin, and I'm here for a Dokkaebi Orb. Your . . . er, house . . . is very, er . . .' she trailed off, and finally managed to say, 'cosy?'

Still terrified, the Dokkaebi backed away. But he soon hit a wall, so he tried to hide the Dokkaebi Orb in his trouser pocket. The glow gave it away instantly. Serin flinched, just as taken aback as the Dokkaebi. Panic hung in the air as she struggled for words, unable to take a step forward.

Then, she spotted something.

A photograph in pieces, lying where the young Dokkaebi had been sitting earlier. Fortunately, one piece was big enough to show an entire face.

Serin made out a large pair of headphones and some freckles. It was Mata, the little Dokkaebi from the Bookshop.

Finally, she realized why this Dokkaebi's name had sounded so familiar. As the Dokkaebi dug furiously into the wall behind him, she said, 'I'm a friend of Mata!'

The Dokkaebi nearly had his head in the wall when he froze. 'You know Mata?'

The Dokkaebi turned, revealing a hint of joy on his face, but for only a moment. Then he struggled to put on a big scowl. 'I-I don't know any Mata!'

But thankfully, the Dokkaebi gave up trying to dig into the wall. He turned his back on Serin, but she could tell that he was listening.

'Haku, listen,' she pleaded. 'Mata still thinks of you as a friend. Even if you're mad at him right now.'

Quietly, Serin waited for a response.

It wasn't long before Haku slowly turned.

'I gave him a present,' he gasped. 'But he tossed it right in the trash. It took me so long to find an empty tin can. It was a hundred and three years old, too, from exactly the year he was born.'

Haku's shoulders were trembling. Serin had to set things straight.

'Haku, Mata didn't realize, that's all. Friends misunderstand friends all the time, right? I saw him just a few days ago, and he misses you terribly.'

'You mean it?'

Serin nodded. 'He says he thought you wanted him to throw away the can for you. Remember? He can't hear very well.'

Haku's eyes widened.

Serin went on, 'Didn't you know that already? I thought you were friends.'

'What? But I . . .'

From his reaction, Haku didn't seem to have known. 'See? You misunderstood him too,' she pointed out, and scanned the cavern. She spotted a large stereo lodged in the wall. 'You know what I think Mata will like better than a tin can? A nice stereo. And if you have something important to tell him, you should write him a card, or a letter. Then he'll understand you properly.'

Haku sniffled and sobbed. 'Th-thank you. You're really kind.'

Taking out a piece of tissue that had clearly seen much use, Haku wiped his eyes and his nose, and held out a sticky hand. 'My name is Haku, but you already know that. I go to humans and I take . . .' He trailed off.

'What do you take from humans?' Serin asked.

Haku blushed shyly. 'I . . . I take rule-following,' he replied, only slightly louder than the footsteps of an ant. Thankfully, he continued in a louder voice, 'I was lonely, okay? So I make people want to do things they're not supposed to do. And I make them not want to do things they're supposed to do.' Then his voice dropped to a whisper as he added, 'Not like you'd understand.'

'No, I understand,' Serin said, curling up just like Haku had when she first found him. 'I know what it's like to be lonely. I don't have any friends, either.'

Haku looked up and opened his mouth, like he wanted to say something, but he seemed to stop himself.

'No, that's not right,' Serin corrected. 'I did have one. My sister Yerin was my best friend, but now she's gone. I have no idea where she is.'

Now it was Haku's turn to try and console Serin. He floundered briefly, then wandered off somewhere.

When he returned, he was holding out a little hairpin with a butterfly sticker. 'Here.'

Serin stared at the hairpin in shock. 'What's this?'

Haku hung his head guiltily. 'I don't just take rule-following from humans. I steal their stuff, too. You know how sometimes you think you put something away carefully but then it disappears? That was all me.'

Haku's head hung so low that he looked about ready to dig under his feet. Serin took his hand before he could try. 'Thank you. This was my favourite hairpin.'

Running a finger over the sticker, Serin said, 'I think I had a huge fight with Yerin after I lost this hairpin. I thought she'd stolen it. We wear the same size and we like the same kinds of styles, so we used to fight all the time over clothes and accessories. I was the one who misunderstood her.'

Serin's eyes reddened, and soon, tears were running down her cheeks.

Haku reached for his used tissue, but stopped and took out the Dokkaebi Orb from his pocket instead. 'Here.'

Sniffling, Serin looked up.

'I'll sell you the hairpin for one gold coin. Then you can have the Dokkaebi Orb, too,' Haku offered.

Serin hesitated. So Haku reached into her pocket and took out one gold coin, setting down his Dokkaebi Orb next to her.

'Thank you, Serin. I would have hated Mata forever if not for you. I'm going to go talk to him right now. You know which way the exit is, right?'

Serin nodded.

'Great! Then see you around!' Haku went over to the hole he'd started digging earlier, but then came right back around. 'Almost forgot,' he said, dislodging the massive stereo from the wall. The cavern trembled, but it did not collapse. 'All right, goodbye now!'

With that, he was gone. The cavern was still holding, but probably not for long. And Serin didn't want to stay much longer anyway. Picking up the Dokkaebi Orb, she scrambled out the way she came.

The wind was howling. It was pitch black outside, with rain hammering against the heaps of junk. There was a roar of thunder, and a bolt of lightning struck a metal rod sticking out of the rubbish.

Serin staggered back in surprise and fell on her backside – and not because of the thunder. For the briefest moment, the lightning had illuminated a towering ink-black shadow in the shape of a spider, almost as large as the heaps of junk.

Slavering and growling, the spider slowly drew near.

Serin wondered which was worse: rushing back into the cavern and getting crushed in the junk, or getting caught and eaten by the monster.

But something leapt in front of her: Issha.

Growing to the size of a wolf, Issha snarled and gave a thunderous roar. The spider froze, its six beady eyes going from Serin to Issha.

Another bolt of lightning struck a nearby heap. As if on cue, Issha lunged. But the spider slapped him away with ease, sending Issha flying into a pile of junk.

There was a terribly clear thud, but Serin couldn't look away, because now the spider had its eyes on her. She scrambled to her feet and tried to back away, but slipped in a puddle and fell again. The spider drew closer and closer, until she could feel its breath against her face. 'Leave me alone!' she cried.

She shut her eyes tight, bracing for the worst.

Nothing happened. Had the spider understood her?

When Serin opened her eyes, she saw Issha with his jaws clenched around the spider's hind leg. The spider tried to shake him off in irritation, but Issha refused to give in.

'Issha!'

Realizing that Issha had no intention of letting go, the spider began to writhe violently. The blood from its leg, mixed with Issha's drool, flowed to the ground in streams. Finally, the spider began to bash its own body against the junk heap.

Issha whined, coughing up blood. He fell limp to the ground with one severed spider's leg in his jaws. Sheets of rain washed away his blood, which flowed in Serin's direction. 'Get up, Issha! Stay with me!' she cried.

But Issha did not even twitch. The spider reared, as if ready to fend off another attack, but Issha remained still.

On seven legs, the spider limped towards Serin. But her eyes were still locked on Issha.

'Please, Issha. Get up . . .'

She didn't know if it was rainwater or tears running down her cheeks. The monster was inches from her now, but Serin didn't run. All she cared about was Issha. The spider raised one massive pincer into the air. This was it.

'Worry not, Miss Serin.'

Serin thought she was hallucinating. It must have been rainwater in her ears, or an echo of the rumbling thunder. Or maybe she'd lost consciousness already and was caught in a dream.

She looked up.

Standing before her was a familiar Dokkaebi. The umbrella in his hand concealed his face, but his other hand held a cup of coffee, which he brought to his lips with immaculate calm.

'I can't have one of our esteemed guests getting hurt.'

Serin remembered his voice and gasped. She must not have been the only one taken by surprise, because the spider, too, stumbled and brought its pincer down on the Dokkaebi.

But the statues behind the Dokkaebi were quicker to respond. Easily more than a dozen animals bolted forward, tearing off the spider's legs and puncturing its eyes.

Like an earthworm attacked by ants, the spider crumpled into a heap. In a matter of seconds, it was no longer recognizable.

'Are you all right, Miss Serin?'

A smiling moustache emerged from under the umbrella as Durof turned elegantly.

Episode 16
The Casino

'Thank you, I'm all right,' Serin said as Durof helped her to her feet. 'But Issha—'

Issha lay unmoving on the ground. Half-limping, Serin rushed to his side. The other animals were around him now, licking his wounds.

To Serin's great relief, Issha was still alive, his legs twitching.

'Issha will be fine once he's got some food in his belly,' Durof assured her. 'Please, let us take you back to the hotel so you can rest.'

As soon as she'd laid Issha on the hotel bed, Serin picked up the phone and called for room service, listing off one thing after another before deciding to order everything on the menu.

She lay down next to Issha while she waited, and thought back to everything since waking up at Popo's Garden. It was the hardest day she'd had since coming to the Rainfall Market, and she barely had the strength to lift a finger.

Serin closed her eyes, and before she knew it, she was asleep.

When she opened her eyes again, Serin instantly thought of Issha. Was he all right? Hoping Durof was right that some food would restore him to health, she scanned the room.

Issha was indeed awake and healthy. And the room was a mess of empty plates and platters.

'Issha, did you eat all this by yourself?' Serin asked, looking around and spotting Issha's messy muzzle. She got down from the bed and stepped on a piece of paper. 'Is this my bill?'

She had been so worried for Issha that she hadn't thought about how much her food would cost. The bill went on like a lengthy scroll.

'Let's see here . . . one . . . two . . . three . . .'

Serin gave a relieved sigh as she counted her gold and the prize money from the restaurant. She had just enough to pay for the meal, leaving her with exactly two gold coins.

'Oh right! My Dokkaebi Orb!'

Remembering that she hadn't checked her newest Orb, she made sure it was still in her pouch. If this Orb really did have the life she wanted, she didn't need any more gold coins anyway.

'Please let this be the right one . . .'

Serin barely had enough gold for another Orb, let alone time. The water in her watch had run down so much that she wasn't sure she had more than one or two days left.

'How are you feeling, Issha?' Serin asked, growing desperate. 'Can you show me the Orb right now?'

Issha's tail wagged. He seemed to be doing much better. In a voice so bright he sounded like he'd never been hurt at all, he meowed.

The suite was awash in an orange glow.

The cosy house looked perfect for a small family, except maybe for the patch of mould on the ceiling. They probably didn't get much sunlight in the home.

A pile of toys were heaped in a corner of the living room, and an air conditioning unit was covered in colourful stickers. Although Serin couldn't feel it, a big, soft mat covered the floor.

'Vroooom!'

A little boy was playing with a toy car in each hand, racing them down a balcony that had been converted into a room. The cars soon changed into dinosaurs, then into transforming robots. Each time, the boy yelled a different noise.

The boy was so young and innocent that Serin felt like she'd gone back to happier times, too. She turned to look at the living room.

Her eyes were instantly drawn to a framed wedding photo. A man and a woman, beaming at the camera. Just looking at the happy young strangers put a smile on Serin's face. The bride outshone the gorgeous flowers in the backdrop, and the man looked as though he was on top of the world.

But she soon recoiled.

From inside the bedroom, someone swore.

When Serin peered inside, she found the man and the woman from the photo embroiled in a heated argument.

They were both red-faced, and looked ready to throw punches. The row went on with neither side willing to give in.

Though she had been made up to perfection in the photo, the woman in real life wore no makeup at all. She shrieked, 'Are you mad? Look at this credit card bill! We can't afford to spend like this! Why do you have to be so selfish?'

'I'm doing this for the family, not for myself!'

'You should have discussed it with me!'

Though he had been smiling brightly in the photo, the man now sported deep creases in his brow. His bright smile was gone, replaced by a furious glare and a look of irritation as he retorted, 'How am I supposed to do business if I don't spend anything? How am I supposed to retain clients?'

'I'm not telling you to ignore your clients! But what about me and the baby?' the woman shot back, hands on her hips. Before the man could respond, she added, 'We're paying a fortune in mortgage and car loans every month already!'

'Enough whining! I'm doing my best, all right?' the man snapped.

He threw open the front door and stomped away. The woman stood stock-still, staring at the door. Then she burst into tears.

The boy playing on the balcony, too, began to wail at the top of his lungs, hands still tightly clutching his toys.

Serin emerged from the vision in horror. Then she punched her palm, having realized something. Issha jumped to the floor in surprise.

'Finally, I understand,' she gasped. 'All I needed was money.' She wanted to kick herself for not figuring it out sooner. If only she had, she would have left the Rainfall Market by now and enjoyed the life of her dreams. She was glad to have thought of it before her time was up.

As Issha rolled like a ball on the floor, still full from last night's meal, Serin called him over. 'Thank you so much for everything, Issha,' she said, resolute. 'This is the last one, I promise. I know what I want.'

A massive pyramid towered over them.

The only difference from the pyramids she'd seen in pictures was that this one was made of gold. For a moment, she stood awe-struck at its majesty. If Issha hadn't tugged on her clothes, she might have stood there for hours until her time at the Rainfall Market ran out.

A red carpet led into the pyramid entrance. Feeling like a VIP, Serin let herself stroll elegantly down the carpet. Issha, too, seemed to like the carpet, from the way he kept scratching it.

Under the sparkling neon sign were the suit-clad security guards, their sharp gazes palpable even from behind their black sunglasses. They wouldn't let a single ant into the premises without their approval.

Serin stopped before them, hoping they might see her as a guest, but she wasn't sure. Her clothes were a muddy mess from the scare in the rain the other night. *What if they think I'm a beggar?*

The guards stopped her.

'What is your business here?' asked one of the guards, his barrel chest threatening to burst out of his suit.

'I'm here for a Dokkaebi Orb.'

The guard seemed to look on disapprovingly. Anxiously, Serin reached into her pocket unbidden and took out her Golden Ticket. The guard looked from the Ticket to Serin and back again, then spoke into his earpiece:

'Sir, we have a human at the door asking for a Dokkaebi Orb. Shall we let her in? She has a Golden Ticket.'

The guard waited briefly, seemingly listening to someone's orders on his earpiece, then ended the call.

'One moment, please,' he said to Serin. 'The boss will come to meet you in person.'

It wasn't long before a tall, strapping Dokkaebi emerged from the pyramid, flanked by more guards than the ones around the building. He towered over them all, so intimidating that Serin's knees began to knock.

'You're here for a Dokkaebi Orb, are you?'

But to her shock, his voice was much higher-pitched than she'd imagined. Even his enunciation was poor, making him sound like a deflating balloon.

'Show me your Ticket.'

'Oh, yes. Right here,' Serin said, quickly holding out the Golden Ticket to the tall Dokkaebi. But he did not even blink.

The high-pitched voice said, 'Eyes down here, Missy.'

It was only then that Serin realized the tall Dokkaebi hadn't moved his lips at all. Either he was a skilled ventriloquist, or he was not the Dokkaebi who was talking to her.

Serin slowly lowered her gaze, lower and lower until she

was nearly looking at the ground, and finally found the owner of the voice.

The Dokkaebi was the size of a rat – and looked like one too, with a long nose and protruding front teeth.

The ratlike Dokkaebi put his hands on his hips and fumed. 'Who taught you your manners, Missy? You're supposed to look someone in the eye when they're talking to you.'

The Dokkaebi was making a serious effort to sound dignified, but his squeaky voice was more childish and pompous than anything. Not wanting to offend him further, however, Serin quickly knelt down to meet his gaze.

'I'm so sorry. My name is Serin, and I'm here for a Dokkaebi Orb. Do you know if I could find one here?'

Appearing a little less angry, the Dokkaebi crossed his arms. 'Of course there's one in here. But first, let me introduce myself.' He cleared his throat. 'Gromm Antonio Valteraccion de Gregory III. You'd better not forget it, it's not long at all. I'm the Sleep-Taker. I take away the desire to sleep at night. Causes insomnia, but that's not my problem. It's what keeps my Casino here running twenty-four hours a day. And why not? I deserve it. Won't find anyone more accomplished than me. Won the A for Effort Prize five years running at the Beginners' Gambling Tournament and Brightest Smile Award at the Junior Bodybuilding Competition three years in a row. And I also won . . . what did I win, Frank?'

The tall guard Serin had mistaken for the boss produced a scroll from his suit pocket. When he unrolled it, the end went rolling into the distance.

'Master Gromm Antonio Valteraccion de Gregory III is the winner of the Little Toe Award at the Professional Toenail-Cutting Championship and the Winner of the Small Munchies Prize at the Baby's First Solids Contest. He set records at the

Hands-Free Trouser-Wearing Competition and the Longest-Time-Gone-Without-Showering Contest—'

'I think the human gets the point, Frank,' said the small Dokkaebi. 'Even a dumb-looking one like her. Am I right?'

Serin laughed awkwardly and nodded, but all she remembered from the long spiel was the Dokkaebi's first name, which she was rather proud of considering how much information he had just spewed.

Gromm preened. 'All right, follow me. Much longer in the sun and I won't make it through the preliminaries at next year's Fair Complexion Competition. I'd be a laughing stock.'

Taking out what seemed to be a tube of sunscreen, Gromm slathered a generous layer over his face and led the way inside, followed closely by his guards. Serin trailed along after them.

The Casino looked even more magnificent on the inside. Serin wasn't surprised to see that everything was gilded. The bejewelled ornamentation and the crystal chandeliers almost made the pyramid's exterior seem shabby in comparison.

They made their way down a short corridor and emerged into a hall overflowing with slot machines, each occupied by the people who Serin presumed were the humans who had gone missing, the ones the Dokkaebi at the Restaurant were talking about. They did not turn when she passed by, eyes locked on the colourful fruits on the spinning wheels and hands wrapped around the levers.

'The Casino floor. You *do* have some coins to gamble, yes?' Gromm said pompously, looking up.

Serin reached into her pocket and fingered the two gold coins she had left as she examined the slot machines. To her relief, they accepted single gold coins as payment. She nodded.

'All right, use one of our slot machines and I'll give you the Dokkaebi Orb. Frank!'

Frank brought out a large box and opened it up. Resting atop a silken cushion was a glowing indigo Orb.

With a gulp, Serin went to the closest slot machine. Then she remembered the coupon from the guidebook and inserted it with the gold coin.

At first, Serin had no idea what to do. But a quick glance around the floor told her it wouldn't be too hard. The slot machine was ready. She pulled down the big lever. The wheels in front of her spun wildly, flashing one fruit after another, easily more than twenty kinds.

One by one, the wheels came to a stop. Each displayed a different fruit.

Even Serin could tell that she hadn't won a thing. The machine displayed the message *Better luck next time!* and went dark.

But just as Serin made to rise, the screen flashed back to life, displaying an arrow pointed at the lever. It must have been a bonus game from the coupon.

Without thinking, Serin reached out and pulled the lever. The wheels spun wildly again.

Something was different this time.

'A cherry . . . another cherry . . . huh?'

In huge, bright letters, the screen displayed the word *JACKPOT!* Serin had seen this on TV. Before she could respond, gold coins rained down from the slot machine.

POOF!

A shower of confetti covered the floor, and a live band popped up out of nowhere to play exciting music. People began crowding around Serin, not to congratulate her but to glare enviously.

Before she knew it, there was a small mountain of coins

under the slot machine, more than the money she'd got at the Pawnshop, and more than the prize money from the eating competition.

Once the music had finished, the band rushed away, and the guards stood at attention once more, as though nothing had ever happened.

Only Serin remained frozen, unable to speak.

'Bravo!' Gromm cried, and whistled. 'A jackpot on your second spin! You, Missy, are a lucky young woman.'

Serin was so shocked that she barely recognized Gromm's changed attitude. He looked up at Frank, who was drenched in sweat from dancing to the music.

'See the young lady to the VIP floor.'

'Yes, sir,' Frank replied robotically.

Gromm gestured to the pile of coins on the floor. The guards behind him came forward to collect them into sacks the size of sandbags. Serin had won a total of five sandbags' worth of coins, which were so heavy that the guards struggled to carry more than two at a time.

'Right this way,' said Frank. He led the way with big strides, followed by the guards with the coins. Sandwiched between them, Serin practically had to jog to make sure she wasn't crushed.

They went up the stairs to the first floor.

The first floor was nothing like the one below. Instead of walls were iron bars as high as a person was tall, and the floor was made of thick glass, under which was a massive pool of water.

Serin tiptoed cautiously across the glass, then nearly jumped when she spotted something shaped suspiciously like a shark glide past below. Then she heard a cacophony of growling and barking from beyond the bars.

The only thing that hinted that this place was still the same building as the Casino was the bejewelled desk. It was massive, with a spotlight pointed at the centre.

The guards led Serin to the desk.

'Welcome to the Stage of Death,' said a high-pitched voice. Gromm was sitting in an oversized chair, his feet dangling off the floor. The guards pulled out the chair opposite him for Serin to sit.

Frank came forward with a teapot, filling an entire cup with a drink Serin didn't recognize.

'You must be thirsty,' said Gromm. 'Please enjoy your welcome drink. My special recipe, made with the greed I collected from human hearts.'

As a matter of fact, Serin had been feeling thirsty. She raised the cup to her lips.

'Hiss!'

Out of nowhere, Issha thwapped her hand. Serin nearly dropped her cup.

Frank grabbed Issha by the scruff of his neck. 'Let me get this ill-mannered cat out of your way.'

'It's all right, please put him down,' Serin replied, gulping down the rest of her drink. 'Issha is my friend, and we're not going to be here long.'

Serin didn't notice the even greedier glint that rose to Gromm's eyes. 'Let's begin, then.'

'Begin what?'

'The game, of course. If you can defeat me, I will pay you double your jackpot. But wait!' he paused, and turned to Frank. 'I need to keep my end of the bargain.'

Frank put the box with the Dokkaebi Orb on the desk.

'The Orb you wanted. And if you like, I could buy any other Orbs you have, for a good price.'

Serin shook her head. 'I don't need any more gold. I just want the Dokkaebi Orb so I can leave.'

'Are you certain?' Gromm asked, sounding like he had something up his sleeve.

Suddenly, Serin felt dizzy. She saw two of Gromm, his outline growing hazy, then clearing again. Shaking her head, she wondered, *What's happening? Am I feeling tired?*

But just as she tried to dismiss the dizzy spell, a voice seemed to speak into her head.

You can't be serious. These Dokkaebi Orbs are worthless compared to the Rainbow Orb.

And then, thoughts of the Rainbow Orb came bobbing to the surface, filling her thoughts. Serin needed more gold coins so that she could buy even more Dokkaebi Orbs. She had to get more.

Gromm grinned. 'Shall we begin?'

Without waiting for an answer, he shuffled a deck of golden cards and set six cards on the desk, three for himself and three for Serin.

'For the first game, the player with the largest sum is the winner,' he explained.

Then, Gromm flipped over his three cards.

'Let's see. Six of spades . . . five of clubs . . . ten of diamonds . . . add them all together, and I get . . .' He had to resort to taking off his socks to count past ten, but even that didn't seem to be enough, because he reached over to the guard next to him for one more hand.

Without warning, Gromm's head bowed forward. Then he began to snore.

Serin didn't know how to respond, but the guard calmly sprayed Gromm with a bucket of water.

'Glug!' Gromm gaped, and rubbed his face. He spotted the shock on Serin's face and said, 'Nothing to worry about, Missy. This is what happens when you steal too much sleep from humans. In any case, let's have a look at your cards.'

Once Gromm had added up Serin's hand, he scowled.

'Hmph, that was just a practice match.'

Then he clapped twice, and a pair of guards hauled in a massive roulette wheel and set it down on the desk with such a loud thud that Serin was sure either the wheel or the desk must have broken. The numbers on the wheel went past thirty.

'A simple game. We each choose a number and spin the wheel. Whoever's guess is closest to the number the ball lands on is the winner.'

Once the numbers were chosen, Gromm rolled a small golden ball on to the wheel. It spun and spun and spun until it finally landed in the number next to Serin's. Gromm slammed an angry fist on the table, but barely made a dent.

Loosening his collar, he said, 'Not bad at all, Missy. Not bad at all. But if you win the next game, you'll win four times your original jackpot. Frank! Bring the dice.'

Serin's heart leapt at the new offer. Four times her original jackpot could probably get her every Dokkaebi Orb in the Rainfall Market, and then some. Maybe she really might get her hands on the Rainbow Orb. But Issha leapt on to her lap and began to tug at her clothes.

'What are you doing, Issha? Stop bothering me.'

But he only tugged harder, until Serin was sure he would tear her shirt.

'Issha, I already fed you earlier! It's all your fault I barely have any coins left, I need to get more!'

Issha jumped down to the floor and bit down on Serin's heel.

'Ow! Issha, what is wrong with you? No wonder your last owner—'

Serin clapped her hands over her mouth, but too late. It was obvious what she was going to say. Thunderstruck, Issha looked down, tail hanging low, and backed away – then scampered down the stairs.

'Issha!'

Frank stopped her as she tried to rise from her seat. With a sneer, Gromm said, 'Good riddance, I say. Who needs an ungrateful animal bothering them at the Casino? Back to the game, Missy. Odd, or even?'

Serin didn't feel much like playing any more. She let Gromm choose first.

The dice rolled loudly in the cup, and came out to another victory for Serin.

Gromm must have been furious, because he said nothing and simply looked down, red-faced. He was practically steaming from his ears. One of the guards behind him assumed he'd fallen asleep again and splashed him with another bucket of water. Gromm looked up at the guard with indignation, and the guard bowed so low that his sunglasses nearly fell off. With a wave, Gromm had the guard taken away. Serin heard screaming outside the doors.

'Now,' Gromm said, still seething. 'For the next game—'

'Wait!'

'What?'

'I . . . er . . . I need to use the toilet. That drink of yours was just so good that I finished it all,' Serin said, clutching her belly and trying to look as uncomfortable as possible.

'Frank!' Gromm called, as Frank walked back through the door, shaking out his hands. 'Take our esteemed customer to the toilet. And make *absolutely certain* she comes back.'

To her horror, Serin realized that Gromm's eyes were bloodshot. *He doesn't just want my coins. He wants all of my Dokkaebi Orbs, too.*

I have to get out of here.

Serin followed Frank downstairs. He showed her to a curved passageway leading to the toilets. 'I will be waiting for you here,' he threatened robotically.

'Right,' said Serin, starting off and sneaking a quick look back. Frank was stubbornly rooted where he stood, back still turned. She would have to find some way out through the toilets.

But just as Serin turned the corner, her heart nearly stopped. Someone was walking towards her.

'Durof!'

'Shush!' he hissed, covering her mouth. 'Everything Issha sees and hears is fed back to me, Miss Serin. I believe you might be in some trouble. Please keep your voice down.'

'You have to help me, Durof,' Serin pleaded in a whisper. 'This tiny Dokkaebi is trying to keep me here in the Casino forever.'

'Did you bring Gromm's Dokkaebi Orb?'

'I did.'

'Then I'll cause a distraction. You make your escape to the Hotel.'

Serin nodded. Durof left her in the passageway and turned the corner, where Frank was still waiting.

'Frank, my good man! It's been much too long. I see you've been bulking up even more since we last met, I'm very impressed! Muscles almost as charming as my moustache, if I do say so myself. Are you busy at the moment, by chance? What do you say to a man-to-man conversation, just the two of us? Coffee?'

But even as Durof held up his half-drunk cup, Frank refused to budge.

'I'm on duty, Durof. And did you forget that Master Gromm has blacklisted you? He'll tan your hide if he sees you here.'

'That's the thing, Frank. For some reason, Gromm thinks I cheated, but that was an unfortunate misunderstanding. I'm here to set the record straight. Let me speak to him,' Durof insisted, bodily turning Frank around.

Serin saw her chance. Crouching low, she slipped away.

But just as she made her way towards the entrance, a man at the slot machine next to her swore.

'Damn it all!'

The screen in front of him displayed four different fruits. *Better luck next time!* flashed almost tauntingly in his face. The man cradled his head in his hands, and spotted Serin pass by. Their eyes met.

'You!' he cried. 'You won that jackpot earlier, didn't you? Please, just let me borrow ten coins! No, five! I'll pay you back double on the next spin, I promise!'

Now all eyes were on her again. Including Frank's.

'STOP!'

Frank practically shoved Durof aside as he charged. The guards at the entrance followed suit, surrounding her.

'Oh dear,' Durof muttered with a sigh, and pulled out a statue from his jetted pocket. He whispered an incantation, and suddenly, a fully-grown cheetah was bursting from his hand. Durof mounted its back and bolted in Serin's direction – and not a moment too soon, snatching her a second before one of the guards grabbed her by the neck. Hauling her on to the cheetah's back, Durof manoeuvred the cheetah with unbelievable agility and slipped out of the building.

'No! Get me my Dokkaebi Orb!' Gromm howled amidst the yelling of the guards and their frantic stampede.

But the commotion soon grew distant behind Serin as the cheetah sped onward.

Episode 17
The Dungeon

Serin was panting when she stepped off the cheetah at the Hotel. 'Thank you, Durof. You saved me.'

'Anything for one of our esteemed guests,' Durof replied, putting the cheetah statue back into his jetted pocket.

Serin was too tired to walk to her bed, instead sinking into a nearby chair.

Still standing there, Durof asked, 'Is there anything else I can help you with?'

'Not at all!' Serin said gratefully. 'You've done so much for me already. I'm really grateful, and I think it's time for me to go home. I've had enough adventure, and the rainy season is probably going to end soon.'

But for some reason, Durof remained unmoving. 'There must be something I can do for you, Miss Serin. For instance, show you the contents of your new Dokkaebi Orb.'

'Oh!' Serin replied, clapping her hands together. 'You said you could look into Dokkaebi Orbs too, right? Then would it be all right? If you could help me just one more time?'

But as she held out the Dokkaebi Orb, Serin gasped.

'Durof?'

There was a hint of madness in Durof's gaze, locked on the Orb. Somehow, he scared her even more than Gromm's bloodshot eyes.

'Is something the matter?' Durof said calmly.

But Serin said nothing. Her gaze went from Durof's face to his outstretched hand. To his sleeve.

Durof followed her gaze.

'Hm?'

His exposed cuffs were decorated with rows of shiny golden cufflinks. But one spot was conspicuously empty.

The rest were a perfect match for the ornament left in Mata's Bookshop.

Serin backed away.

'Is something the matter, Miss Serin?' Durof asked, stroking his curly moustache. Then Serin remembered something else.

Durof's moustache was so long that if he stretched it out completely, it would be as long as a Dokkaebi woman's hair.

And as the realization dawned on Serin, Durof began to look less and less friendly.

'Is something the matter, Miss Serin?' he repeated, taking a sip of his coffee.

Then Serin saw the steam rising from the cup and remembered what Toriya had told her.

A smoking Dokkaebi! Toriya didn't see smoke, he saw steam!

Serin tried to back away further, but she was too exhausted. Her legs gave out.

Durof finally dropped the act.

'Hand over your Dokkaebi Orbs, Serin. I'd rather not waste my energy here.'

Serin trembled. 'It was you . . . you were the one breaking into those shops . . .'

Durof did not give excuses. Instead, he threw back his head in laughter. 'Aha!' he clapped. 'Bravo, Serin! A clever deduction, yes! Pity you weren't more clever, because then you might have handed over your Dokkaebi Orbs earlier.'

He smiled, his perfect white teeth glinting. But somehow, there was no affection in that smile, and his eyes were glowing with hunger.

Serin had to get away from Durof. Since her legs refused to budge, she willed her arms to push her backwards.

But like a hunter toying with his prey, Durof easily kept up, taking one step forward for each of her awkward pushes. It was hopeless.

'Issha!' Serin finally cried. 'Help me!'

Again, Durof burst into laughter. 'Looking for this?'

In his hand was a small cat statue, the very one Serin had seen at the Information Desk at the start of her journey.

'What a silly young lady you are, Serin. First you say you don't need him, and now you beg for his help,' he snickered, one hand on his forehead.

Then, to Serin's shock, he held out the statue to her.

'Then again, I suppose he does belong to you. Please, take Issha back.'

Serin couldn't risk Durof changing his mind. She reached out to grab the statue.

'Whoops!' Durof said, singsong, and dropped the statue. It fell to the floor.

Then he kicked it, hard.

The statue hit the wall and shattered into a thousand pieces.

Issha was gone. Serin went limp.

'Ah, my apologies. It seems I've neglected to properly introduce myself,' said Durof, fixing his already-perfect suit jacket. 'I am Durof, the Self-Esteem Taker. A pleasure to have made your acquaintance.'

Durof's hand took on an eerie blue glow, and suddenly, a cloud of blue emerged from Serin's chest and was pulled into Durof's hand.

With all the grace of an English gentleman, Durof placed

one hand over his chest and gave a deep bow. 'And now, I bid you good night.'

And then, Serin wanted to sleep.

She was so exhausted.

Where am I?

When she forced herself awake, Serin found herself in complete darkness. All she knew was that the floor was almost too hard to sit on.

With a gasp, she reached into her pockets. As she'd feared, the pouch with the Dokkaebi Orbs was gone. She was left only with the second pouch, filled with useless shopping from the Rainfall Market.

She breathed a heavy sigh, then inhaled. 'Is anyone here?'

But no one answered, except the echoes of her own voice bouncing against the walls she could not see.

Then something occurred to her. Serin rummaged through the Dokkaebi pouch she still had – and found what she wanted.

The candle of encouragement from Nicole's Perfumery. With a pack of matches considerately taped to the bottom.

There was a hiss, and the wick caught fire. Serin held up the bright light, trying to make out her surroundings – an empty, walled-off space that was more a large corridor than a room. She decided to explore the area, but the more she walked, the more she got the feeling that she was going in circles. With each step, she felt more and more miserable.

Finally, Serin stopped and plunked to the ground. She felt stupid for feeling hungry at a time like this.

Then she remembered the garlic bread from Bordo and Bormo, and rummaged through her Dokkaebi pouch. Luckily, the bread was still soft and fresh. A heavenly smell greeted her nose as she pulled the loaf out of the pouch, and Serin bit right in. She hadn't eaten in so long, and the good food made her drowsy. She did not resist when sleep came.

A man she'd never seen before looked down at her proudly.

'Look at those little legs, she's got quite the kick! She might grow up to be a football player. Some kind of athlete.'

The woman next to him gave a wry chuckle. 'Honey, she's only a baby. Don't pressure her already.'

But the man only grinned, looking even more determined. 'You never know, she just might do it!' He met Serin's gaze, and in his deep, clear eyes she could see her infant self.

'Serin,' said the man, 'whatever you decide to do with your life, sometimes you'll run into obstacles that make you want to give up and leave. But if whatever you're doing is something you're absolutely sure about, don't give up, you hear me? I have faith in you.'

The man gave the baby a gentle kiss on the cheek. His wife took the baby's tiny hand in hers and wrapped her arm around her husband.

I can't do it, Dad. I'm hopeless.

Serin stirred. The memories she thought she'd put away were rushing back now, filling her thoughts—

How they all laughed at me.

How we couldn't even afford a new school uniform.

How I was never any good at anything.

No matter how hard she tried, she never seemed to make a difference.

All the encouragement in the world was no help at all.

Then came a voice:

'Is someone there?'

Serin looked up. The voice was loud, loud enough to drive

her thoughts away. Then came footsteps, many of them, and Serin had to rub her eyes in disbelief.

There stood the elderly man she had met outside the Rainfall Market. He, too, recognized her. 'Young lady! It's you again!'

Serin gaped for a moment before she finally found her voice. 'I . . . sir?'

The elderly man took another step forward. Now they could see each other better.

'I was worried about you when you disappeared at the Pawnshop, Miss! To think you were here all along. Are you all right?'

Serin wanted to say something, but her throat was tight and she knew that if she spoke, she would burst into tears. So she simply nodded. And noticed other people with the elderly man.

She recognized those faces.

At the front of the group, holding a lit lighter, was the university student who had been turned down at his job interview. Next to him was the woman at the successful company, then the café owner, then the civil servant who wanted to be free, and the travel writer who drank away his sorrows.

They introduced themselves one by one, though Serin already knew them all.

She explained what had happened to her, as concisely as she could, and they did the same. Her candle was halfway gone by the time they were finished.

'The sleazy Dokkaebi with the moustache is behind all this. He's the mastermind,' someone said, and everyone cursed in agreement.

'How do we get out of here?' Serin asked hopefully.

'We've already searched this place thoroughly,' said the elderly man. 'But there was only one exit, and . . . well . . .'

Serin waited, so desperate that she forgot to blink.

'There's a terrifying Dokkaebi standing guard there. Armed with a massive club,' the elderly man finished, wiping sweat from his brow.

All hope was lost. Serin could see it in the others' faces, too. No one said it, but it was obvious that everyone was ready to give up. Serin, too, resigned herself – until she remembered something.

'Will any of this help?' she asked, pulling out her crumpled Dokkaebi pouch. Everyone looked at her incredulously, and a few people even gave hollow barks of laughter, but Serin quickly opened up the pouch and shook it out.

'What is all this?'

Despondence turned to curiosity as her shopping emerged into the light. Everyone stepped closer to the candle, and that somehow made them look a little more hopeful.

Huddling together around the pile of things, the people began to murmur – then they broke into discussion, their hopes renewed.

Meanwhile, Serin and the elderly man went off to the side. They still had more to discuss.

'I've seen all these people,' Serin said to him. 'I saw their lives in the Dokkaebi Orbs.' As the elderly man listened, she added, 'And the last Dokkaebi Orb I found was supposed to be full of money and wealth . . . Was that your life?'

As Serin waited tentatively, the elderly man nodded.

'It probably is.'

Now Serin was even more curious. 'Then why on earth would you want to come to the Rainfall Market?'

The elderly man smiled. 'To find the happiness I didn't have.'

'You mean there was something you couldn't buy with money?'

'Of course,' the elderly man replied with a glance at their huddled companions. Then he met Serin's wide eyes. 'What I wanted more than anything else was youth – to be young again, just like you. All the money in the world couldn't turn back time. Tell me, young lady. Do you have treasured memories?'

The question took Serin by surprise. 'Like what?'

'Memories that you can go back to when you feel down. Memories that make you happy. As it happens, I don't have any of those. I wasted all my years doing business, always with my nose to the grindstone, and never made the time to make happy memories.' He sighed deeply. 'I never realized that some things are infinitely more precious than wealth. If only I could be young again, I would spend more time with my loved ones.'

Serin fell into thought. And she remembered the times she'd shared with Issha. Their memories together.

We ate Nicole's carrot cake together and got cream all over our faces.

We wove in and out between the mischief-trees to pick their fruits.

We won the eating contest and left a handprint and a pawprint on the wall together.

Each recollection was a precious, priceless memory.

Serin wanted to see Issha again. She burst into tears.

'I do have good memories,' she sobbed as the elderly man listened quietly. 'I met this cat here. His name is Issha. He – he helped me find the Dokkaebi Orbs. But then I said something horrible to him, even though I knew how much he'd already suffered.'

The elderly man offered a handkerchief. It was soft and clearly expensive.

And it had a rainbow pattern. Serin gasped mid-wipe.

'I-is something the matter?' asked the elderly man.

But Serin simply stared at the handkerchief. It was only a few seconds later that she finally managed to reply, 'I think I know why Durof took my Dokkaebi Orbs. And . . . and maybe why he trapped us here.'

She pulled out her guidebook and opened it to the first page.

'What do you—'

Before the elderly man could finish, the others were crowding around. They must have finished their strategy meeting, because one of the men said in a steely, determined voice, 'We have an idea. It's not perfect, but it's all we've got.'

Serin and the elderly man gave him an urging look.

'Serin, we're going to use the things you brought to make a trap,' a man suggested. He had a mop of messy hair and small eyes that made him look a little tired. The stretched neck of his T-shirt and his yellow joggers seemed to suggest he'd just rushed out of bed, and the big cartoon elephant on his shirt and the toe socks peeking from under his sandals made a strong, if not necessarily good, impression. His toes were wriggling constantly.

All the others, Serin had seen already in the Dokkaebi Orbs. But this man was a complete stranger. Someone explained that he'd been caught trying to sneak into the Chief's quarters.

'But to do that,' the man continued, 'we need someone to bait the Dokkaebi standing guard.'

He looked around, but no one met his eyes.

Serin raised a hand. 'I'll do it.'

Everyone looked up in shock, but no one was more shocked than Serin herself. Until a few minutes ago, she'd thought she was hopeless. But at some point, she began to feel that she couldn't keep running away. That she had to dig in her heels. She glanced at the scented candle, whose wick was almost completely gone. She finally remembered what the candle was called.

'Are you sure? This could be dangerous,' said the man.

'Don't worry,' Serin replied confidently. 'I'll outrun him. I know I can.'

The man nodded. 'All right, then. I'll take you to the guard. Everyone else, please make sure the trap is set.'

The guard Dokkaebi was not far off.

With a borrowed lighter in hand, they followed the passageway until they hit a dead end. A flaming torch burned against the wall as loud snores rumbled across the room.

'There he is.'

The man pointed at a Dokkaebi in the distance – larger than a human man but smaller than Toriya – who had dozed off with his club propping him up. He looked almost as ferocious as Dunkie.

Behind him was a metal door.

Suddenly nervous, Serin trembled.

'It's all right,' the man said, noticing her hesitation. 'You don't have to force yourself, we can find another—'

But Serin stepped forward. 'No. I can do this. I just have to lead him back to where we were, right?'

Her foot hit a rock on the ground. Serin picked it up and lobbed it as hard as she could at the sleeping Dokkaebi. It flew in a straight line and hit him square in the nose.

With a grimace, the Dokkaebi opened his eyes. And Serin took a deep breath.

'Hey pig-face! Yeah, you! I heard your breath smells worse than your wind! I bet all the Dokkaebi girls can't stand being near you!'

Serin had only said what had come to mind, but from the way the Dokkaebi bared his filthy yellow teeth, at least part of her guesses were probably true. Especially the last accusation. He glared daggers as he stomped forward.

'I-is that good enough?' Serin asked her companion, unsure.

The man replied, equally uncertain, 'I think you might have insulted him a little too well. Let's get out of here.'

They bolted together into the darkness, towards the trap the others had set.

Luckily, the rest of the group had finished preparations. As Serin rushed over, they waved her quickly to the side, gesturing at her to stick close to the wall. Her foot narrowly missed a puddle on the ground, and she didn't have time to ask what it was before the guard Dokkaebi came stomping, his yellow teeth glistening.

The others staggered back in terror, but not as far as Serin had expected. They had a plan.

As the Dokkaebi lunged, he stepped in the puddle and slipped dramatically, landing flat on his back. The crash was so hard that Serin almost worried that the floor might collapse under them. But the Dokkaebi seemed to be just as strong as the floor, because he slowly got back to his feet. Serin tensed, ready to run.

But the other people's gazes were locked on the ceiling.

Serin looked up. And her jaw dropped.

The travel writer was near the top of the wall, holding Serin's Dokkaebi pouch. Supporting him was what seemed to be a long stick – the bamboo that Popo the gardener had given Serin, now grown to enormous length.

The writer climbed further until he was directly over the Dokkaebi's head. Then he shook out Serin's pouch, dropping a hefty tome corner-first on top of the Dokkaebi.

There was another dull thud, and the Dokkaebi fell once more. But this time, he did not stir.

When Serin and the others drew closer, they realized that the Dokkaebi was foaming at the mouth, completely out cold. With muffled cheers, they climbed over him. Serin joined the crowd, trying not to step on the unconscious Dokkaebi.

'Look, everyone! We're almost there!'

Without warning, the people in the lead stopped.

They had a big problem: the door was locked, and no one had the key.

Episode 18
The Lounge Bar

The man at the head of the group kicked the metal door. He tried to shake the handle. But the door refused to budge. An uneasy murmur spread through the group. Someone suggested going back to the unconscious Dokkaebi to see if he had the key, but no one volunteered to take that risk.

Meanwhile, the man at the front peered into the keyhole. 'It doesn't have to be the key,' he said. 'If only I had something like a metal wire . . .'

He turned around without thinking, and nearly screamed when he saw Serin. She nearly screamed back. He had noticed the butterfly-shaped hairpin in her hair, and she had realized who he was. The author of the book she'd read about the Rainfall Market. The keyhole had pressed a dark, round mark around his eye, which suddenly made him resemble the doodle-scarred face on the front flap of the book.

'Wait, are you—' Serin began, but the man snapped, 'Give me that hairpin, now!'

Still stunned, Serin handed over her hairpin. The man unfolded it and stuffed it into the keyhole. Now Serin knew this was indeed the author who had been in and out of prison multiple times.

There was a brief but clear *click*.

The door screeched open, and at the first sight of escape, the people finally cheered out loud.

'Let's be off!' the elderly man said, patting Serin on the

back. She did not need any encouragement to follow the others out of the Dungeon.

They spotted a light in the distance – the doors Serin had seen when she first set foot in the Rainfall Market. Other than the conspicuous absence of dancing Dokkaebi, the hall was exactly the same as it had been at the time, with the exception of the water hourglass. The top half was running nearly empty.

Luckily, the doors out of the hall were unlocked. Everyone rushed through, one by one.

And like before, Serin and the elderly man, standing at the back of the crowd, were the last. He stopped when he realized that Serin was hanging back.

'Is something wrong, young lady?'

'You go ahead, sir. I still have business to take care of.'

For a moment, the elderly man seemed confused. Then he asked, 'Is it because of that cat you told me about?'

Serin nodded.

The elderly man met her eyes and smiled. 'It's good to be young. I wish I had half your courage, young lady. Be careful, and make sure you escape before the clock runs out.'

With that word of encouragement, the elderly man slipped out the doors. The sound of Serin's footsteps echoed all alone in the hall as she rushed to a lift she'd seen on her way to the hall. She knew where she would find Durof.

'Oh no.'

Pasted on the lift doors was a sign that read OUT OF SERVICE. She tried pressing the darkened buttons and slapped at the doors, but to no avail. Serin sighed and stared despondently, ready to give in.

Then she spotted a blinking light next to the lift. A sign for an emergency stairwell.

The stairwell door screeched when Serin pushed it open, as though no one had used it in decades. Once it was open enough for her to pass through, Serin saw stairs. Stairs that seemed to go on forever.

Can I really do this? she wondered. But not for long.

Serin rushed up the stairs, her every step filled with determination.

Durof hummed to himself as he boarded the lift, holding the Dokkaebi pouch Serin had got from Mata. He pressed a button, and the lift slowly ascended.

Then, as soon as he'd stepped out on the top floor, he broke the lift with ease. As the lift crackled and sparked, he made his way to his destination, the sound of his footsteps echoing across the narrow hallway.

At the end of the hallway, Durof stopped. Hanging elegantly in front of him was a smart sign that read *The Lounge Bar*. And on the door handle hung a crooked sign that read, CLOSED.

Durof gave a scowl and kicked the door open. The lounge bar was empty and cold.

'I suppose a relaxing drink with our esteemed chief was too much to ask,' Durof said.

'Don't worry, you'll have your hands full with me,' someone replied from the shadows. 'Give you a bit of exercise for once.'

Sitting at one of the tables was Berna, holding a glass of liquor.

And hanging above, an enormous spider.

The spider slowly descended and landed next to Berna, its six eyes glinting.

'Please, Berna,' Durof replied, pulling his statues out of his pockets. 'I doubt I'll even break a sweat.'

back. She did not need any encouragement to follow the others out of the Dungeon.

They spotted a light in the distance – the doors Serin had seen when she first set foot in the Rainfall Market. Other than the conspicuous absence of dancing Dokkaebi, the hall was exactly the same as it had been at the time, with the exception of the water hourglass. The top half was running nearly empty.

Luckily, the doors out of the hall were unlocked. Everyone rushed through, one by one.

And like before, Serin and the elderly man, standing at the back of the crowd, were the last. He stopped when he realized that Serin was hanging back.

'Is something wrong, young lady?'

'You go ahead, sir. I still have business to take care of.'

For a moment, the elderly man seemed confused. Then he asked, 'Is it because of that cat you told me about?'

Serin nodded.

The elderly man met her eyes and smiled. 'It's good to be young. I wish I had half your courage, young lady. Be careful, and make sure you escape before the clock runs out.'

With that word of encouragement, the elderly man slipped out the doors. The sound of Serin's footsteps echoed all alone in the hall as she rushed to a lift she'd seen on her way to the hall. She knew where she would find Durof.

'Oh no.'

Pasted on the lift doors was a sign that read OUT OF SERVICE. She tried pressing the darkened buttons and slapped at the doors, but to no avail. Serin sighed and stared despondently, ready to give in.

Then she spotted a blinking light next to the lift. A sign for an emergency stairwell.

The stairwell door screeched when Serin pushed it open, as though no one had used it in decades. Once it was open enough for her to pass through, Serin saw stairs. Stairs that seemed to go on forever.

Can I really do this? she wondered. But not for long.

Serin rushed up the stairs, her every step filled with determination.

Durof hummed to himself as he boarded the lift, holding the Dokkaebi pouch Serin had got from Mata. He pressed a button, and the lift slowly ascended.

Then, as soon as he'd stepped out on the top floor, he broke the lift with ease. As the lift crackled and sparked, he made his way to his destination, the sound of his footsteps echoing across the narrow hallway.

At the end of the hallway, Durof stopped. Hanging elegantly in front of him was a smart sign that read *The Lounge Bar*. And on the door handle hung a crooked sign that read, CLOSED.

Durof gave a scowl and kicked the door open. The lounge bar was empty and cold.

'I suppose a relaxing drink with our esteemed chief was too much to ask,' Durof said.

'Don't worry, you'll have your hands full with me,' someone replied from the shadows. 'Give you a bit of exercise for once.'

Sitting at one of the tables was Berna, holding a glass of liquor.

And hanging above, an enormous spider.

The spider slowly descended and landed next to Berna, its six eyes glinting.

'Please, Berna,' Durof replied, pulling his statues out of his pockets. 'I doubt I'll even break a sweat.'

Loudly crunching ice cubes with her teeth, Berna met his eyes. 'The little tussle at the Scrap Yard was barely a real fight, do you hear me? I was only supposed to get the Orb from the girl and keep a watchful eye on you back then. This time, I'm prepared.'

She snapped her fingers. Swarms of spiders crawled out of the darkness under the chairs and tables, surrounding Durof.

Completely unperturbed, Durof replied, 'Then you know what I came for. And that you stand no chance of stopping me.'

'I know that you stole those Dokkaebi Orbs and brought them here. I know you're going to use them to make a Rainbow Orb. Or have you already finished?'

Durof applauded theatrically. 'Excellent detective work, Berna! Bravo! And no, I have yet to produce a Rainbow Orb. That can wait until I have the Chief sitting before me and his heart stops in shock as I craft the very thing he has forbidden!'

Sneering, Berna retorted, 'You'd be lucky if he blinked once. The Chief has always known how ambitious you were, Durof. That's why he ordered me to keep tabs on you. He knows that you chose humans to invite to the Rainfall Market, and how you used the spirit creatures to show only specific snippets of the lives in the Dokkaebi Orbs. There's only one thing you're doing before the Chief, and that's getting on your knees to beg forgiveness.'

Durof hung his head, shoulders trembling. It almost looked as if he were crying.

Then he threw back his head and laughed.

'Berna, Berna, Berna!' he sang. 'How long must we continue to toil under a dying old man? How long must we remain helpless, fated to be cursed the moment we take a handful too much from human hearts? When I gain the power of a Rainbow Orb, I will become the new Chief and bring about a new world, one where the Dokkaebi need no longer live in hiding!

A world where we rule, damn the old man! I am sick of playing concierge, do you hear me?'

Berna put down her unfinished glass. 'I've had just about enough of your madness,' she hissed.

'I didn't think you would understand,' Durof replied. Then he recited a spell, bringing his statues to life.

'I could say the same for you,' said Berna. She made a casual gesture, and the spiders, big and small, charged forward.

Then there was a deafening explosion.

Serin looked up. The noise had come from somewhere close.

How much further do I have to go? she wondered. She had long since stopped counting the floors, which had been difficult to begin with since the landings were unmarked and looked completely identical. If she hadn't been so used to climbing stairs on her way home from school, she would never even have considered coming up this far.

Luckily, she spotted a small door only a little further up.

'Please be the top,' she whispered, and tugged at the handle.

On the other side, she found pure pandemonium.

The Lounge Bar's sign was in pieces, and seemed to have flown all the way down the lengthy hallway to the lifts. The establishment's door was reduced to splinters and exposed the inside of the bar. What unfolded inside was a strangely familiar sight.

Shadowlike spiders and stone animals of all shapes were tangled in battle. The spiders looked exactly like the one Serin had seen in the Scrap Yard, only smaller, and the animals were the same ones too.

And standing calmly in the midst of it all, clad in a purple suit with a cup of coffee in hand, was a Dokkaebi Serin knew all too well.

'Durof!'

He was too far away to hear her, but Serin called out anyway. She bit her lip so hard that she tasted blood.

Durof's gaze was locked on a pile of broken dishes and silverware. He was so intent on the rubble that he did not seem to notice Serin at all. There was a weak moan from under the heap: Berna.

'I don't need a Rainbow Orb to defeat the likes of you,' Durof said confidently. He smiled, noting that his animals were overpowering the spiders.

Then his eyes landed on the doorway. And met Serin's gaze. Nearly dropping his coffee cup, he stumbled briefly, but quickly gathered himself with practised grace. 'My, my! I must admit, this is quite the surprise, Miss Serin,' he said.

'Give back those Dokkaebi Orbs,' Serin replied. 'I'm going to save Issha.' She surprised herself with her own confidence, even taking the candle into account. The Lounge Bar fell silent.

Durof stared, dumbfounded. It was like he didn't comprehend Serin's statement.

Then he threw back his head and roared with laughter, clutching his gut and rolling on the floor. He was in such a fit of laughter that he might laugh himself to defeat.

Unfortunately, he soon recovered and got back up. 'How utterly terrifying,' Durof said, not sounding terrified in the least. He wiped the corner of his eye with a handkerchief and added, 'Do take him back . . . if you can.'

He raised his hands into the air, leaving himself defenceless. But Serin could not take another step, because his animal statues, still made of stone but very much mobile, were gathering around him. Their teeth dripped with spider pus, looking almost like blood.

Then, dozens of sets of fangs turned on Serin.

Episode 19. The Penthouse

Serin stood frozen in the doorway. The effect of Nicole's candle must have run out, because she could feel her knees knocking.

Durof, on the other hand, smiled and took another step forward. As did his stone animals.

'Miss Serin, when you received your invitation, you might have asked yourself: "Why me?"'

He paused dramatically, and added:

'I did not choose you because you were special. Heavens, no. I chose you because you were the most useless human whose story I had the displeasure of reading.'

Serin clenched her fists, but no more. She knew that nothing she did could frighten Durof.

'No money. No talent. Not a single person to call a friend.'

Durof burst into laughter again.

'Resourceful man that I am, I decided to make use of your useless nature somehow. Squeeze value out of nothing.'

With the pride of a mathematician who had just solved a centuries-old problem, he explained:

'I would make you bring me the Dokkaebi Orbs I needed to create a Rainbow Orb. It was no easy task, dyeing the right Dokkaebi Orbs to complete a set of seven in the colours of the rainbow. If you had strayed once from my carefully scripted plans, I would have used Issha to hypnotize you into my bidding – but fortunately, there was no need for that. You played your part to unwitting perfection.'

He pulled out the Dokkaebi pouch from his pocket.

'And now, you have granted me my dearest wish.'

Then Durof raised his hand, and his stone animals poised to strike.

'As thanks, I will make certain that your end is quick and painless.'

The animal statues inhaled. So did Serin. It was hopeless now. All she could do was close her eyes and wait for the end.

Then, there was music.

An upbeat melody came echoing down the hallway. At the same time, Berna weakly looked up from the pile of rubble and smiled.

'So many guests today.'

Marching down the corridor behind Serin were a host of familiar faces.

Holding hands at the very front were Mata and Haku. Strapped to Mata's back was the massive stereo Serin had seen at the Scrap Yard, blasting music from the speakers.

'Durof! You stay away from our friend!' Mata demanded in a shockingly loud voice.

'Are you all right, Serin?' asked Emma, who had just recovered from tripping on a piece of the Lounge Bar sign.

'Durof! You'll pay for all those explosions in my shop!' Nicole warned, a can of stink spray in each hand.

'Se . . . rin . . .' Toriya enunciated, carrying Popo on his shoulder. The purple flower Serin had picked for him stuck out of his front pocket.

Serin stood in stunned silence as the Dokkaebi came forward and stood protectively before her.

'What is the meaning of this?' Durof demanded, breaking into a cold sweat. He took a step back, and his animals seemed to hesitate.

'How dare you threaten the poor girl?!' howled Panko,

winding up a gigantic toy monkey – one of multiple large wind-up toys he had set up in the blink of an eye. As soon as he set the monkey on the floor, it clapped its cymbals loudly and charged – then tripped and fell forward.

A cloud of dust rose into the air, and everyone began coughing. Durof saw his chance.

Stepping back, he pulled out a second Dokkaebi pouch, from which he produced a small book.

A book precisely the size of the one stolen from Mata.

'I suppose I have no choice,' Durof muttered, flipping to the page with the Song for the Rainbow Orb. It was only a second before his slimy voice filled the ruined Lounge Bar.

'Hey, I know that song!' Mata cried.

One by one, the Dokkaebi Orbs in Durof's possession rose into the air and shone with blinding light. Then they lost their colours and floated together, merging into one rainbow-hued Orb.

As though guided by a string, the Rainbow Orb slowly came to rest in Durof's hand.

'Finally . . .' Durof gasped, holding the glowing Rainbow Orb with reverence. Then his whole body flashed with the same light as the Orb.

A moment later, the glow dimmed into a dark aura pulsating from Durof himself. He gave a wicked grin.

'Now it's time to test the power of the Rainbow Orb,' Durof remarked.

He pushed his hand into the air. The entire roof was blown away. 'My, my,' he exclaimed, and then pushed towards the wall. The wall came crumbling down, exposing a magnificent Penthouse.

Teeth glinting whiter than usual in the sunlight, Durof sneered. 'Even the Chief would deign to show his face if I destroyed you all. I do wonder how much more powerful my statues will become once I've filled them with my new power.'

Then he held out his hands towards the fallen spiders. Tendrils the colour of ink spilled from Durof's palms, pulling the fallen spiders together and fusing them into one clay-like mass. The mass became a boulder, which then stirred into the form of one gigantic spider.

The new spider was bigger and even more horrifying than the one that had attacked Serin in the Scrap Yard. The stone animals, Serin and her friends might be able to overcome. But she didn't know how they would stand up against this huge spider.

Cold sweat beaded on the brows of the other Dokkaebi, and Panko in particular was positively drenched. Serin could feel her newfound courage seep away.

'NO ONE MESSES WITH OUR EATING CHAMPION!'

A roar that could give a loudspeaker a run for its money resounded off the ruined walls, breaking the tension in the air. Another group of Dokkaebi arrived, each one practically the size of a house.

The Dokkaebi leading the group carried a flower-print ladle in one hand and was picking his nose with the other.

'Bordo!'

Next to him was a Dokkaebi with rogue chips hanging from his beard and a Dokkaebi with the biggest scowl on his face.

'Hank! Dunkie!'

'Sorry we're late, Bordo got us all lost,' said Bormo, who was holding a massive skillet. 'But I guess we haven't missed too much.'

The giant Dokkaebi brandished their silverware and kitchen utensils, and except for Hank dropping his tankard, they made for an intimidating show. Now Serin and Durof were evenly matched.

Durof seemed taken aback at the stream of reinforcements, but was not deterred. He had a Rainbow Orb in his grasp, which gave him more confidence than ever. The dark aura around him made it clear that he could probably go for days without food or sleep.

'No matter,' he said. 'I can think of no better targets on whom to test my new powers!'

The Orb in his hand spewed a cloud of darkness. The spider stirred, and the animals growled and barked with even more ferocity.

Serin's friends were not intimidated. Nicole showered herself in special perfume and took aim with her stink sprays, while Mata raised a large tome over his head. Next to him was Haku, ready to throw his tin cans. Emma took a determined breath and pulled out a pair of nose hair scissors from her apron, then quickly put them back and pulled out an electric saw instead. Panko, too, was busy at work fixing the fallen wind-up monkey, which quickly came back to life.

'Destroy them all!' Durof commanded, and chaos descended on the ruins of the Lounge Bar.

Another cloud of dust rose into the air as Dokkaebi, statues and a giant spider tangled in the rubble. Toriya punched away the stone animals two at a time, and Popo made an ineffectual but valiant attempt from his shoulder with her walking stick.

Mata and Haku worked together in perfect sync. When Mata smashed an animal statue with one of his impossibly hefty tomes, Haku would follow up with a barrage of tin cans.

Panko, too, did surprisingly well, whipping around a skipping rope and using it to choke a statue that drew too close. The wind-up monkey had not yet toppled, tirelessly clapping away on unsuspecting animal statues that wandered between its cymbals.

But most brilliant of all was Emma, who struck down statues with each effortless swing of the saw, sending fragments of rock flying. She would have done better as a warrior than a hairdresser, all hint of clumsiness gone.

Yet the efforts of the Dokkaebi combined did not seem to have much of an effect, because Durof magicked more and more statues to life.

Even as the giant Dokkaebi from the Restaurant grabbed the spider by its legs, the spider held its ground and swiped at the Dokkaebi with its free legs. Neither side was winning yet, and it was hard to tell if anyone had the advantage.

As the battle raged, Serin found herself stepping back. She wanted to do something to help – anything – but there was nothing she could do in a fight like this.

I chose you because you were the most useless human whose story I had the displeasure of reading.

Bile rose to Serin's throat. Durof was right. She was utterly useless.

The more she inched away from the battle, the closer she got to the edge of the ruined Lounge Bar. She was so anxious that she failed to notice Durof emerge from the ongoing melee, drawing near with a tune on his lips. As Serin watched Panko's already-large nose swell after taking a hit from a statue, Durof leaned close.

'For you, Miss Serin, I have a special gift,' he said.

Serin flinched. She was not one to turn down a present, but she would never trust a gift from Durof. He didn't seem to care.

Durof reached into his jetted pocket.

The moment his hand emerged, Serin nearly screamed.

'I couldn't be bothered to piece him back properly, but who

knows? Issha may surprise you and me yet,' he said, dripping with self-assurance. 'For you, Miss Serin, I now fill him with the rest of my magic.'

An incantation escaped Durof's lips. The statue glowed, then swelled.

'Issha . . .' Serin gasped.

The creature that emerged from the statue was not the Issha she knew.

Standing before her was a horrible, slavering beast.

Episode 20
Issha the Guide Cat

Issha's face was a stitched-up mess, sparks and black smoke escaping from the gaps each time he breathed. The smoke was intensely hot, as if straight from the fires of hell.

But in spite of it all, Serin somehow knew it had to be Issha. Bared fangs and all. Somehow, she was not afraid.

Hot tears ran down her cheeks.

'Issha!' she pleaded. 'It's me, Issha. It's Serin. Don't you recognize me?'

Issha only growled.

Howling with laughter, Durof said mockingly, 'Miss Serin, I'm afraid Issha is no longer the sweet, lovable guide cat you knew. He is a weapon. A weapon I will use to conquer the human world.'

Durof couldn't have been more correct. Issha didn't have to demolish buildings or eat people alive to scare Serin, because the very sight of him was terrifying.

But she took a step forward anyway.

'I'm sorry,' she said, as Issha growled ferociously.

Durof gave an amused chuckle. 'I see you've lost your wits, poor thing. Any last words before Issha devours you whole?'

Again, Serin did not retort. Her eyes were locked on Issha as she strode on.

'I'm sorry, Issha,' she said. 'I should never have said those awful things to you. I didn't mean any of it, I promise. Please believe me.'

Finally, Issha was within reach. Serin placed a hand on the bridge of his nose. He snarled threateningly.

'I'm sorry I hurt you, Issha. You don't have to forgive me if you don't want to. But I wanted to apologize anyway. Those days we spent together were the happiest times of my life, and I'm sorry I took it for granted until it was too late. I guess I didn't have what it took to be a good friend to you.'

'Finish her!' Durof commanded impatiently. 'We do not have *time* to waste on this useless creature. We have a Chief to overthrow and a whole world to conquer. We will take revenge on the humans who abandoned you to starvation.'

Issha gave a heartrending cry, his voice resounding across the ruins. Serin, Durof, and the Dokkaebi fighting further away were all forced to cover their ears.

As the horrible roar faded, Issha lowered his head completely. Plumes of black smoke came spewing from his body as he grew smaller, going from the size of an ox to his true form – a small kitten.

'Useless beast!' Durof spat, snatching at the smoke but only managing to grasp a few of the escaping strands of magic. 'You gluttonous, stupid creature!' he howled, and kicked the weakened Issha.

Issha went flying. He hit a collapsed wall and landed in a corner without so much as a squeal.

'No!' Serin cried, rushing over with tears streaming down her face.

Channelling the remainder of the magic he'd retrieved from Issha, Durof levitated a long piece of plywood into the air.

'Now it's really time to end this,' he said, raising the plywood higher into the air until it was perfectly poised to strike Serin. 'I suppose you didn't have long anyway, as the rainy season is all but over, but I would like to do the honours myself.'

As tendrils of smoke wrapped around the plywood, Durof said one final word:

'Goodbye.'

The plywood flew like a missile at Serin, who could only stand over Issha, completely cornered. Durof did not even need to see what would come next. He turned.

With an awful *crack*, the plywood shattered. And Durof burst out laughing.

Though the battle was still raging around him, the odds were turning in his favour. Emma's saw was almost completely blunted, and Mata's tome had been reduced to a cover with no pages. Panko had run into a wall and lost consciousness after his glasses were broken. Toriya's face was blue with bruises, his dear purple flower trampled to paste in the frenzy of fighting. The giant Dokkaebi, too, had mostly been defeated and knocked out cold. There would be no more miracles.

'It's over,' said Durof.

No one could stand against him now. The Penthouse was within reach. He held out the Rainbow Orb to retrieve the power he had given to the animal statues.

Then he doubted his ears.

'Issha is *not* a gluttonous, stupid creature!'

Standing behind him was someone who should not have been standing: Serin.

Lying in front of her was the piece of plywood he had thrown, split cleanly into two boards.

'How—'

'Issha is the best eater in the world!' Serin cried, taking a single step back into a stance Durof had never seen before.

'And you know what else?'

She added:

'He's my precious friend!'

Then Serin turned, spinning into a perfect kick that hit

Durof square in the jaw. Before he knew it, Durof was flying – knocked off the ground – and then he was falling headfirst, and landing with a loud *smash*. He rolled across the floor, but quickly got to his feet.

'How *dare* you?' he demanded with a ridiculous squeak, having broken his two front teeth. He reached forward to retrieve the power of the Rainbow Orb – and realized that his hand was empty.

He had dropped the Rainbow Orb in the fall.

Almost simultaneously, Durof and Serin lunged for the fallen Orb.

Durof was a little faster. His hand was inches from the Rainbow Orb now, and Serin was still too far away. He grinned triumphantly.

But when he grasped, his fingers touched nothing but air.

Issha had recovered, and leapt forward to snatch the Rainbow Orb away. With the Orb clutched in his jaws, he stood midway between Durof and Serin, looking from one to the other.

'Issha!' Serin cried.

'There's a good boy, Issha,' Durof cooed with a fake smile, creeping forward as Issha hesitated. 'I have been your master all these years. Now listen to me and bring me the Rainbow Orb.'

Now he was close enough that one easy leap would close the distance. Durof made ready to pounce.

'Issha! Eat the Rainbow Orb!' Serin yelled.

'No!' Durof screamed.

Their voices reached Issha at the same time, but Issha only listened to one.

The Rainbow Orb went down Issha's throat and took on a bright white glow as it went into his stomach. Issha slowly rose into the air, and it was clear to all that the Rainbow Orb had a new owner.

There was a powerful impact. Durof fell on his backside, turning away from the brilliant light. Serin, too, was tempted to look away, but refused to take her eyes off Issha.

Somehow, it looked like he was telling her goodbye.

Issha disappeared into a pillar of light, which instantly pierced the clouds and disappeared into the sky. Soon the light was a star in the distance, clearly visible even under the sun.

And then he was gone.

Serin remembered Issha's wish. *He's been reborn.*

Then she heard a heavy *thud* and turned. The enormous spider that had tried to crush the giant Dokkaebi had fallen. Then Durof's animal statues began to crumble one by one, and soon only pieces of stone and exhausted Dokkaebi were in the ruins of the Lounge Bar. Serin was the only one standing, until she was not.

Without warning, the Penthouse doors slowly creaked open.

A large, silhouetted figure emerged, flanked on either side by servants.

It was clear to Serin that this Dokkaebi was very old indeed. It was also clear exactly who he was.

Episode 21
The Treasure Vault

'Chief Yan!' Berna cried, confirming Serin's suspicions. The Chief and his servants approached at a snail's pace.

Serin soon understood why. Yan was so old that he seemed barely capable of standing. His face was all wrinkles and age spots – and fatigue, too.

'Chief!' the other Dokkaebi cried as they regained consciousness, falling to their knees one by one.

The Chief could barely take a few steps before he was panting in exhaustion.

'Chief! You mustn't overexert yourself,' Berna advised, even though she looked much worse off than him.

The Chief gave a gentle smile and said in a barely audible voice:

'*Halaa morr nell.*'

Serin didn't understand his words, but guessed that he meant to say that he was all right.

Then the Chief raised his hand, and a beautiful glow erupted from his palm.

The light enveloped Serin and Berna, then the other Dokkaebi in the ruins. Serin could feel her wounds mend themselves. Even Berna rose to her feet, dusting herself off. She rushed towards the Chief but made a quick detour, smacking the consciousness out of a trembling Durof, before taking a knee in front of the Chief.

'My humblest apologies, sir. I only wanted to spare you the effort of concerning yourself with this matter.'

The Chief shook his head. Then he pointed at Serin.

'*Torr beuu deliaa.*'

Berna looked at Serin as well. 'The Chief wants to speak to you,' she explained.

'M-me?' Serin replied with a gulp. Berna nodded.

The Chief was easily twice Serin's height, and something about him radiated majesty, making it hard for Serin to look him in the eye. She found herself staring at her feet as she approached.

'*Bereuenn mohaa ktokk jann nirhaa.*'

'The Chief wants to know your wish,' Berna interpreted.

'I . . .' Serin fell into thought.

As a matter of fact, she did have a wish in mind. She thought it through again, and no matter how much she tried, she could not come up with anything better. Finally, she managed to speak.

'Please give me people in my life who love me as much as Issha did.'

'*Honoo?*'

'Are you sure?'

Serin mustered all the courage in her heart to raise her head and look the Chief in the eye. She nodded.

The Chief turned and looked at the Penthouse. Then he held out one weary hand, and the floor began to vibrate.

A heavy door at the very back of the Penthouse rumbled open. Beyond were riches beyond Serin's wildest imagination. Jewels, gold and silver, and more Dokkaebi Orbs than she could count, all arranged neatly in shelves.

The Chief gestured again, and one of those Orbs was pulled into his hand.

Then he placed the Orb into Serin's hands.

'But—'.

Serin couldn't finish her sentence. And not because she was intrigued or disappointed.

She knew this Orb. It was the very one she had left with the Pawnshop on her first day at the Rainfall Market, still wrapped in her flower-print handkerchief.

Serin looked up. The Chief replied as though having read her mind:

'Zamoo deuu rakuntraa.'

'He says that this Orb contains your wish.'

Serin stood rooted to the spot, awestruck. The Chief took one laborious step forward. Then he placed a hand on the Orb and whispered something in that same incomprehensible language.

But this time, Serin didn't need Berna to tell him what he meant.

'Druu epp zulaa.'

A woman was washing dishes in what looked to be a restaurant's kitchen. From her face, she seemed to be in her forties, but her white hairs had gone undyed, making her look much older. She was stubbornly bent over the sink, polishing the dirty dishes without looking up once.

An older man who seemed to be her employer entered the kitchen.

'Ms Kim, I thought your daughter was starting school today. You should go and see her off like all the other parents.'

As it happened, the woman was working on the last of the plates. She quickly pulled off her rubber gloves and thanked the man profusely as she prepared to leave.

Then the man stopped her and held out a white envelope.

'It's not much, but think of it as a bonus, Ms Kim. Maybe get yourself some new socks,' he said.

The woman looked down at her feet. She wore cheap sandals and a pair of socks that had clearly been darned many times over, but still had holes in them.

Again, the woman thanked her employer and rushed out of the kitchen. She pulled off her apron in a hurry and picked up her bag, and scurried out – running into one of the servers in the process.

'Watch it, lady!' the server hissed, and the woman apologized profusely before rubbing out food stains from her clothes. It wasn't perfect, but the woman looked up at the clock and practically sprinted out the doors.

She soon made her way to a secondary school. Hanging above the front gates was a banner that read, OPENING CEREMONY – WELCOME TO OUR 37TH CLASS OF STUDENTS. *Another banner, which must have hung there longer, listed the prestigious universities that the school's graduates had been accepted to. From the sheer number of names she recognized, the woman supposed the secondary school was an excellent one for clever students. She found herself smoothing out her clothes as she walked through the gates.*

The athletics field in front of the school building had been converted to a car park for the parents that day, filled with luxury cars the like of which the woman had scarcely ever seen. No one was getting out of the cars, which probably meant that she was the last parent to arrive. The woman briskly headed to the auditorium.

Luckily, the ceremony had not yet started, and the woman spotted the child she was looking for – a girl with short hair, standing in the distance.

The woman pushed through the crowds to reach her, but then she overheard something:

'Where are your parents today, Serin?' a man who seemed to be the classroom teacher asked the short-haired girl.

The girl paused briefly before answering, 'They're on holiday abroad.'

The teacher seemed to see through her lie instantly, but did not pry further and gave the girl an encouraging pat on the back.

Unable to bring herself to get closer, the woman stopped. Someone bumped into her shoulder, but she barely resisted. Then a voice came over the speakers announcing the start of the opening ceremony and asking everyone to take their seats.

But the woman turned and walked away.

She slipped out of the auditorium and the school, still covering the stubborn kimchi stain on her shirt with her cheap red handbag.

The woman went immediately to the bank, which was not particularly busy because it was so early in the day. She handed the white envelope from her employer to the teller, alongside her bankbook. When the teller returned the bankbook, the woman smiled.

Written in neat, tidy letters at the top were the words: Serin's University Fund.

The scenery changed once more.

A girl about the same age as the short-haired one from the opening ceremony stood fixed to the pavement. Considering the time of day, she should have been in school, but the girl stood before a clothing store, scrutinizing a school uniform in the display window. Next to her was a skinny girl of a similar age, but half a foot taller.

'Do you feel like going back to school?' asked the tall girl, blowing bubble gum.

The shorter girl scoffed. 'As if,' she snorted, but her eyes were locked on the uniform. 'Go ahead. Gotta take care of something. What's that book you've got, by the way?'

'Apparently it's popular,' said the tall girl, holding out a book titled The Wishseekers. *'Wanna read it?'*

'Maybe later.'

The tall girl gave her a look, then dashed off to the crossing to make a green light. 'All right, see you later.'

The shorter girl waved and watched her friend cross the street and disappear. Only then did she step into the store.

'Welcome,' the tailor said, holding a measuring tape. The tailor radiated courtesy and kindness. The girl returned the greeting and looked around the store. Suits of all kinds hung neatly from the hangers, and the old tailor gave her a gentle smile.

'I . . .' the girl said hesitantly, 'I'd like to buy a school uniform.'

'I see,' replied the tailor, 'this way, please.'

Taking the girl to the mirror, the tailor took her measurements and asked for the name of her school. When the girl answered, the tailor went to the back of the store and asked, 'And what name would you like embroidered on the tag?'

'Kim Yerin,' the girl said, but then stopped herself. 'I mean, Kim Serin, please.'

'A gift, then?' the tailor asked, recognizing exactly what the girl wanted.

'Yes, for a friend.'

'You must treasure this friend dearly,' the tailor remarked.

The girl closed her eyes and fell into thought. The tailor waited patiently, sensing that the girl needed some time in silence.

After a while, the girl gave a surprisingly short answer:

'Yes. She's my best friend.'

Then Serin was back in the Rainfall Market. But she could not bear to look up. Tears ran down her cheeks and dripped down from her chin.

Before she knew it, she was surrounded by Dokkaebi giving her reassuring pats on the back.

'It's time to go.'

Only then did she look up, tear-streaked cheeks and all.

'Thank you, everyone,' she managed.

Emma took her hands in her own. 'We're the ones who should be thanking you, Serin.'

'Take care, okay?'

'The Market wouldn't be standing if not for you.'

'I already ate, thank you. I'll join you some other time,' Mata said bluntly, but Berna covered his mouth.

'It'll take us a while to clean up, but hopefully you'll come visit again.'

'Bye-bye.'

'Safe travels.'

'Get yourself home, now.'

As the Dokkaebi showered her with farewells, Serin said farewell back to each and every one. She wished she could spend more time with them, but she didn't have long. The water hourglass had nearly run its course, reduced to one last fading drop.

The Chief waited patiently all the same, and only when that final drop of water was reduced to a pinprick did he recite an incantation.

'Goodbye, everyone.'

Serin began to glow.

Slowly, she faded from the Rainfall Market, vanishing feet-first. She did her best to burn the faces of her new friends into her mind.

But as she blacked out, she heard Berna's voice, almost hazy in the distance.

'Since we'll be doing repairs anyway, the Chief wishes to make a change. He proposes that we name our establishment after the rainbow, a symbol of hope that follows the misery of rain. All in favour of the new name, the Rainbow Market?'

'Aye!' the Dokkaebi cried in unison.

Serin's eyes fluttered open.

Did I just dream all that?

Nothing seemed to have changed since she reached the

run-down house on the first day of the rainy season. The only difference was that it was now dawn.

A moist wind caressed her face and filled her lungs with fresh air.

Serin stared blankly at the brightening sky, eyes locked on the distance – on the clearest, brightest rainbow she had ever seen, stretching across a cloudless sky.

She was so captivated that she barely realized that she was holding something. A small orb wrapped in a quaint old handkerchief. Slowly, she unwrapped it.

The little orb was just as empty as it had been the moment she first received it.

But Serin was far from disappointed. She held the orb close to her chest, as though cradling the most precious treasure in the world.

The sky grew brighter and brighter, and soon the glassy orb reflected the rainbow in the sky, etching its magnificence in its smooth surface.

Episode 22
The Rainbow

'I'm impressed, Serin. You're improving by leaps and bounds,' said the taekwondo master, nodding as he walked past Serin practising her kicks. 'Were you off doing special training?'

'You could say that,' Serin said vaguely. As the master paused to watch, the other students, too, stopped what they were doing.

One of them was the boy Serin liked.

'Hey Serin, what's your secret?'

'Huh?'

'You know, like do you do some special training?'

'Oh,' Serin said, realizing what he meant.

The boy asked, 'Are you doing a different regimen?'

'Well . . . you see . . .' Serin stammered, but finally worked up her courage. She wanted to be truthful. 'I live really high up, so I have to climb a lot of steps.'

Thinking for a moment, the boy asked, 'Do you live in a penthouse?'

'No,' Serin corrected. 'I live on a big hilltop, with lots of steps to climb.'

The boy still looked confused. She needed to be clear.

'You know, the hill they're trying to redevelop.'

'Oh!' the boy exclaimed in recognition.

Gaze falling lower and lower in shame, she went on to explain: 'It must have been good training climbing up the hill every day. Sorry it's not a cool new training regimen.'

But the boy looked nothing short of serious as he replied, 'No, not at all. That sounds like great training. Do you mind if I join you after class today?'

'What?' Serin gaped, looking up.

Obliviously, the boy chirped, 'All right, I'll see you later!'

Serin was utterly stunned, her face turning beetroot. She quickly turned her gaze out the window.

With a gasp, she realized that the dark blanket of clouds had cleared, ending an interminable downpour.

And as though answering a promise, a rainbow hung across the sky.

Serin remembered a marketplace, and the friends she'd made there. A smile rose to her face, but she didn't know if it was because of the boy, or the memories that came flooding back.

A beam of sunlight filtered through the window and perched on her shoulder.

'I'm home,' Serin announced as she walked through the door.

Her mother looked up from darning a sock and asked, 'Serin, are you expecting a package?' and pointed at a box next to the shoe cabinet. 'It's addressed to you, but there's no sender on the label.'

Serin picked up the box and turned it over curiously.

'It's very light,' her mother added. 'I think it might be clothes.'

'Oh!' Serin exclaimed. 'I think it's from a friend.'

'Really?'

Knowing exactly what she would find, Serin said confidently, 'Yeah. My best friend.'

'I suppose you have a lot of friends I don't know about,' her mother said with a confused tilt of the head. But just as Serin chuckled in response, her mother pushed up her reading glasses and asked, 'What is that over there?'

'What?'

Serin followed her mother's gaze to the front door, which remained ajar.

A small kitten pushed its way into the gap.

'Where'd this kitten come from?' her mother wondered. 'Do you think that pregnant cat a few weeks ago gave birth?'

Serin remembered how she'd handed pieces of melon to a pregnant stray. Her mother picked up a broom to shoo the cat away, but paused.

'How awfully strange.'

'What do you mean, Mum?'

'This kitten is acting just like a dog. Look at him wag his tail.'

'Huh,' Serin replied, only half-listening. She was completely enraptured by the kitten, which was now clambering over Serin's feet, shoes and all, and rubbing against her ankles. She could barely hide her delight, but her face soon fell.

'Mum?' she asked. 'I couldn't keep him, could I?'

To her shock, her mother replied, 'I suppose it's all right, as long as you keep his litter box clean.'

'You mean it?' Serin squeaked, so loudly that her mother jumped. 'Thank you!' Although she got a brief scolding for nearly giving her mother a heart attack, Serin had the biggest smile in the world plastered across her face.

'Now we just need to figure out a name,' said her mother.

'I know what I'm calling him.'

'Already?'

Finally taking off her shoes to enter the house proper, Serin took a seat next to her mother and picked up a needle and thread to darn the rest of the sock. 'Mum, I think life is kind of like a sock with holes in it.'

'Is it now? Look at you, sounding all grown up. You could teach me a thing or two,' her mother teased. 'So why *is* life like a holey sock?'

With a faint smile, Serin replied, 'It's because we mend the holes with our loved ones. Right, Issha?' she asked, turning to the kitten. He had already made himself at home in an empty box, as if he were the king of the household that had just adopted him.

And as if he understood, Issha gave a long cry.

'Meooooow.'

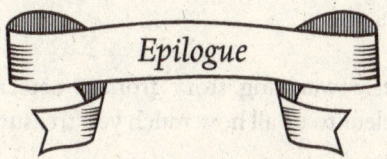

Epilogue

Now for our next segment: Stories from the Listeners.

Today we have a story from a secondary school student who's chosen to remain anonymous. Let me read you her message:

Hello.

I'm the new owner of a lovely kitten. A girl with dreams of joining a taekwondo demonstration team.

I'm not expecting my letter to get chosen, but thought I might write anyway.

My family is not well-off, but my mother is the world's best seamstress, and my little sister, although we're far apart for now, is the sweetest friend I could ask for.

I've always been too embarrassed to say it, but I just wanted to let them know how much I love them both.

I started taekwondo a lot later than most people, and some of the neighbours think it's ridiculous for a girl to learn how to kick and punch.

But I want to join a taekwondo demonstration team and prove them wrong.

I still have a long way to go, but if I keep doing my best, I'm sure I'll make my dream come true. I really hope it will.

Now I don't know what I'm trying to say with my story. I suppose it's a good thing my dream isn't to become a writer.

But I'm going to put in a song request anyway, since you never know if you don't try.

P.S. I'd also like to say hello to all the friends I met during the rainy season.

What a heartwarming story from a determined young woman. It's clear to us all how much you treasure your family and friends.

You said you started taekwondo late, but the truth is, it's never too late to start on your dreams. The present is the best time to launch yourself forward.

Hey, maybe there's a connection there! The 'present' isn't just a moment in time, it's also a precious gift!

Anyway, it's time to play the final request of the night. Sit back, close your eyes, and enjoy 'A Tomorrow Better Than Today'.

> *It may feel like it's raining,*
> *But don't forget that*
> *Behind dark clouds there's sunshine shining*
>
> *It may seem hopeless,*
> *But don't forget that*
> *Behind failure there's always opportunity*
>
> *It would seem that everything is over,*
> *But remember that*
> *The end is a new beginning.*

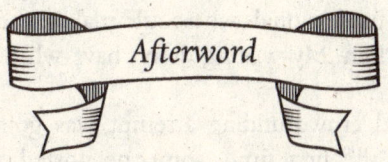

Afterword

'We don't believe your writing has what it takes for publication.'

This was the first line of a response I received to a mass email I sent out long ago to a list of publishers, with my poorly written manuscript attached. At the time, the response broke my heart. Looking back, however, I came to be grateful for that response. I began to wonder what it meant for a piece of writing to be good enough for publication, and frequented bookshops and libraries at every opportunity.

Even now, I don't understand why I chose writing, of all things.

Was it because I happened to have a novel in my hand when I hid behind the gymnasium in middle school to avoid being bullied by delinquents? Or was it because of the powerful memories of being rejected by my university of choice, and spending my hours wandering between comic book cafés and book cafés? Or maybe it was because years of studying for the civil service exams came to nothing, and I consoled myself reading at a small library in my neighbourhood? Whatever the reason, my peers were starting to give up on their dreams when I began to consider a new one, and writing gave me renewed purpose in life.

But not having majored in creative writing or taken formal writing lessons, it was hard to suddenly pick up a pen and write. My first blind crowdfunding attempt received no attention at all, and the book I published independently didn't sell a single copy and was returned by all the bookshops. I tried applying to contests, but my name never made the list of finalists. To make matters worse, I lost all my savings while searching for professionals who could make my book a reality. It was true, then. My writing didn't have what it took to be published.

My second crowdfunding attempt was going to be my last. But for the first time, someone posted a response. I remember crying my eyes out in gratitude. I wanted to repay my new readers for their encouragement, and so found myself sitting at my laptop once more. And with a notebook in hand, I came up with one idea after another – be it in the underground or a corner of my usual coffee shop.

What kind of book did I want to write? Something that left readers with a lingering sense of warmth even after they turned the last page. A light, fun read that was still packed with meaning. A book that could heal wounded hearts and cast a ray of hope into the darkness. That would be perfect, I thought. And so this book was born.

The third round of crowdfunding I started got more love and attention than I'd expected. Though publication issues led to a total reprint of the book at one point, things eventually got resolved with the support of my patrons, who sent encouraging comments and reviews. I even got an official deal with a publishing house after years of rejection. This whole process, I think, will stay with me for the rest of my days.

This book would not have been possible without the help of countless people.

First, I would like to acknowledge the more than 900 patrons who gave me their trust and provided funding for this book. Second, I would like to thank president Youn Seng Hun of Clayhouse, who secured rights deals with multiple prominent international publishing houses before the Korean edition was officially published, as well as editor-in-chief Kim Dae Han, who was always there to support me in my frequent bouts of worry and anxiety. I would also like to thank book designer Sim A Kyung for overseeing the design and publication process, illustrator Jedit for the incredible cover art, and Gong-gan Corporation CEO Son Hyeong-seok for the production of the book.

Above all, I would like to thank my friend Se-jin, who gave me the courage to write when I was hopeless and dejected. Se-jin, you were always there to cheer me on, and even the landscape of the Rainfall Market was inspired by the dream you told me about. It was thanks to you that I could keep on writing even as I juggled call centre and delivery work, and at last managed to complete this manuscript.

Finally, I would like to thank my beloved family and the readers who picked up this book. Although they may not always be obvious, we all live with fears and worries. If anyone reading this message is going through dark, difficult times, I hope my story has given you some small encouragement. Even when the future seems utterly hopeless, when you feel like you're all alone in the world, I have faith that each and every one of us is dearly beloved to someone else. May the dreary days of rain soon give way to a brilliant rainbow arching high across the sky for us all.

I hope that my book will be the Rainbow Orb that points you towards the light you seek.

You Yeong-Gwang

On a station platform, with nothing to read,
and a four-hour train journey stretching ahead of him...

That's where the story began for Penguin founder Allen Lane.
With only 'shabby reprints of shoddy novels' on offer,
he resolved to make better books for readers everywhere.

By the time his train pulled into London, the idea was formed.
He would bring the best writing, in stylish and affordable
formats, to everyone. His books would be sold in bookstores,
stationers and tobacconists, for no more than the price
of a ten-pack of cigarettes.

And on every book would be a Penguin, a bird with a certain
'dignified flippancy', and a friendly invitation to anyone who
wished to spend their time reading.

In 1935, the first ten Penguin paperbacks were published.
Just a year later, three million Penguins had made their
way onto our shelves.

Reading was changed forever.

—

A lot has changed since 1935, including Penguin, but in the
most important ways we're still the same. We still believe that
books and reading are for everyone. And we still believe that
whether you're seeking an afternoon's escape, a vigorous debate
or a soothing bedtime story, all possibilities open with a book.

Whoever you are, whatever you're looking for,
you can find it with Penguin.